ALICE

ALICE

ALLEDRIA HURT

MOCHA MEMOIRS PRESS

Rock Hill, SC

ISBN: 978-1-7352195-6-1

Cover Art by Taria Reed
Editor: Nicole Givens Kurtz
Proofreader: Susan H. Roddey
Publisher: Mocha Memoirs Press

OTHER MOCHA MEMOIRS HORROR TITLES

Dead Heat
Ren Thompson

Black Magic Women: Terrifying Tales by Scary Women
edited by Sumiko Saulson

An Improbable Truth:
The Paranormal Adventures of Sherlock Holmes
edited by A.C. Thompson

The Grotesquerie
edited by Eden Royce

CHAPTER ONE

Thirteen Street

NO NORMAL PERSON RUNS LIKE THAT.

Sunset. Ethan hated the pumpkin orange glow for how it made everything harder to see. Truthfully, sunset made Ethan nervous. Maybe it was the zombies.

Ethan reached up to wipe sweat from his forehead. He'd been hiding in the 13th Street bus for most of the day. It wouldn't move because the back axle was broken, but it made a good lookout spot. It was close enough to the ground to make getting down into the tunnels easy, but high enough the murder wouldn't get to him if he climbed to the top.

What he would do once he got to the top, he couldn't say, but that was the escape plan if he should ever become trapped and unable to get out the door.

Ethan's eyes burned with fatigue.

The creatures moved around more in the night, but that didn't mean they were like bats or owls. Zombies didn't need to sleep. They didn't need to shit or anything, except feed.

With a far quicker motion than brushing away the sweat, Ethan adjusted his scope.

The first one shuffled into view. These things had two speeds: the slow shuffle of traditional zombies or the Olympic

1

sprint of the ravenous. Their usual mode was the slow shuffle conserving energy to chase down dinner. Once they knew food was nearby, they ran and could run for a long time. Ethan had never seen anyone outrun a zombie. A number of people had tried. The quote went: Death was swift.

They moved like geese, a slowly widening v formation forcing things before it. At least, that was what he normally saw. But ahead of him, this murder moved oddly. Shifting his scope again, he keyed in on the disturbance. Something ran *through* the group.

Ethan adjusted his scope again. *That couldn't be right.*

Nothing ran through a murder.

He still had time before they were close enough to *scent* him. Eager for a better view, he crawled out the window and on top of the bus. He laid out flat and tried to get a bead on things from his new position.

A person ran through the zombies, carrying someone else. The zombies behind chased them. The ones in front hadn't turned around to the humans racing toward them. It was weird. The fact only half of the murder seemed to know what was going on only made things much stranger.

"Hey!" Ethan did not bother with his signal code before talking to his teammates. "You seeing this?"

"Oak Ave 101 confirms," Roger said. He stuck with the proper protocol. An old hat who had no use for those who let their training go because of excitement. "Unknown running through the murder. Seems to be a normal person."

"No normal person runs like that!" Ethan said.

"Agreed. "Roger's response left him wondering if the old man was going to shoot at the runner.

The first shot went off. The runner suddenly jigged to the right, putting herself in a zombie's reach. It grabbed her jacket. Without losing her cargo, she snatched free and vaulted over the top of the zombie in front of her. Then she skipped from one shoulder to the next, walking on the shuffling bodies before their running brethren could knock them over.

Another shot split the air and Ethan about swallowed his tongue when once again, it missed.

"Yes," said Ethan.

"Damnit." Dale interjected into the conversation; she was stationed just past Roger's position. "Bitch's fast. Think she's on our side?"

"If she's not, you think it will matter?" Roger's pragmatic response threw a bucket of cold water on Ethan's enthusiasm.

"Good point." Both Ethan and Dale admitted in unison.

"Headed straight for your position, Spotter," Dale said.

Not that anyone thought those creatures out there could remember who they dealt with from one second to the next. Handles were just one of those leftovers from having the former military types running reality. They seemed to have this need to label positions rather than people and to call daily things "Operation Stay Alive". The mission name really was not inspiring at all, in Ethan's opinion.

"I can see that, really, Dale, I can," Ethan said forcing his breath past his *thudding* heart. Then with a motion he'd only seen on television back when the NBA Playoffs were a big deal, she jumped and landed on the top of the bus. Even Jordan didn't have ups like that.

She placed her passenger down next to him and said," Watch him."

With that she dropped off the side.

"Alice." Horror encapsulated in one word. The man she left behind held his arms out to her.

It disturbed Ethan. He'd seen looks of fear like the man's before, but only on children. This guy was not a child.

"Alice!" He called her again.

"Shut up, James," the woman called back.

Ethan heard her clear over the moaning and groaning of the now running dead. They didn't need air to make noise, but then again, they didn't need air to run either.

The zombie stink hung thick in the air. There was no getting used to it because it was always fresh and pungent. Ethan once thought they would eventually stop stinking, but that wasn't the case with the walking dead.

The sound of bones breaking interrupted Ethan's thoughts. He peeked over the side of the bus to spy Alice killing zombies with her bare hands.

Her movements were quick and tended to kill more than one creature at a time. Shoving skulls together, using one body to break another. He even saw her reach through a chest cavity and pull a spine through the front before using it as a whip against the next one. It was *amazing*.

"Spotter, what the hell do we do? Should we shoot with her in the zone?" asked Roger.

Ethan looked to James, who heard the question. Their eyes met. It was then Ethan noticed James's eyes were mismatched brown and blue. They were clear and lucid. Then he shook his head 'yes'.

"Yes, take your shots as you find them," Ethan said.

They couldn't let the murder get away. They would make more.

Minutes stretched as they always did in fire fights. This murder consisted of about a hundred. One hundred lost souls, formerly family members and productive members of society.

By the time the last one finished twitching, the sun had set and the moon had yet to rise. They were left only with the twinkle of the heartless stars above to illuminate the world. Artificial lights worked like bug zappers for zombies. They drew them in. No one used them topside unless they intended to fight the possible murder.

Fighting another murder was not on Ethan's list of things to do. Along with Dale and Roger, his shift was over with sunset.

Alice's return happened like her original appearance, a quick motion and then she was there. Her shirt had once been white. Now it was, in turns, red and brown. Whether or not the brown had once been red, he could not be sure, but there were places where the white still seemed to show through. Alice had some physique to show off as well. Muscles well defined, long limbs, pretty, her eyes were mismatched as well. Not the same as James's but rather hazel and green. It was strange to look at.

"A trick of the light," murmured Ethan ducking his head to avoid staring.

"Your friends need to shoot better," Alice said.

That was the second time Alice spoke in Ethan's direction. She didn't talk to him, but rather *at* him, and she expected him to listen.

"Spotter." Dale's voice cut through Ethan's earpiece. "Safe to come down?"

"Yeah, this murder's down. Best make for the tunnels quick," Ethan replied before switching his radio off. "Hi Alice."

James had crawled over to Alice and wrapped one arm around her leg. She reached down and put a hand on his hair.

"You shouldn't fight them," James said.

"They are not us, James, we've been through this." Alice's voice warmed when she spoke to James. "They can't be us. Besides, they're vermin. Only fit for killing."

Her fingers stroked James's hair and he looked up at her with a worried expression, but it soon warmed into a lopsided smile. She leaned over and put her arm around him, hefting him bodily.

"We'd better get out of here," she said. Then they both looked at Ethan. "Where are we going?"

"We?" Ethan swallowed. She smelled of blood and looked like an ax murderer. Memories of how she'd treated those zombies did nothing to help. "You can't come with us."

"We can't stay out here." The statement sounded like it should answer everything. It didn't, but it sounded like it should. "There are more coming."

Roger stood at the base of the bus and looked up at them. "Central said 'bring them'."

Central was run by a para-military group responsible for the planning of most everything involving the two hundred refugees.

Ethan slid off the bus and landed in a crouch, looking at the older man. Dale came around the edge of the bus with her pistol drawn. A pistol wouldn't keep the zombies off for long, but it would be enough to buy two seconds to shimmy down the ladder and into the sewer where the group kept their home. Ethan looked up, expecting Alice and James to still be standing on the top of the bus. However, they weren't. Instead, she stood a few feet away, having shifted James to his arms around her neck. Her eyes moved over the no longer twitching bodies of the murder.

Many thought moving up into high rises was the ticket. It was workable, except that going up in a high rise meant a questionable amount of food. You had to come out eventually and if the murder made it past the defenses, what were you going to do, learn how to fly? Down below the city, you had more room to run. Not to mention, the smell of sewage masked the scent of human a little bit.

Or maybe that was just Ethan's wishful thinking.

"Whatever y'all are gonna do, maybe we should get to doing it now?" Dale scanned the shadows on the far side of the street.

"You sure Central said bring them?" Ethan asked.

"Getting old, kid, not going deaf. Let's go before the smell attracts more."

Dale moved with slow shifting steps toward the manhole cover and reached down where the control latch was. When the latch was pulled, the manhole cover popped up on its quick working hydraulic. They had a minute before it would snap shut just as quick. It lopped off arms if a zombie managed to get a hand in before the soldier could escape. On more than one occasion, it had cut off heads as well.

"Come on." Dale urged the bunch of them.

Alice jogged over with James on her back and once it was her turn, she lowered him down first.

"Grab the ladder," Alice said.

James did as he was told and lowered himself down using only his arms. Alice just dropped off the side and landed in the muck at the bottom once the landing space cleared. Then she picked James up, paying no attention to the sticky brown smears joining the drying and darkening blood already coating her limbs. She watched the group with her mismatched eyes, waiting for someone to decide what direction they were going. Ethan watched her with wide eyes. There was something weird about the both of them. Very, very weird.

Roger took off down the tunnel with quick strides, taking Dale with him, leaving Ethan to make small talk with Alice and James, who might have been more of a child than a man.

"Stop staring at me." Alice snapped at the wall.

A rat scurried away as if it were the object of her possible wrath. James snickered, bringing one muddy hand up to cover his mouth. The look from his companion made him stop.

"Are you mad at me?" James asked.

Alice gave him a confused head tilt before shaking her head. Her shoulders made a movement as if she were going to shrug, but she didn't. His weight was apparently enough to keep her from being able to do that.

"Then why are you making ugly faces?" James asked.

"We'll talk about it later."

Ethan wondered when later would be. Just from the few minutes he'd spent with her, he already felt Alice not being the type to discuss her feelings. That just made it stranger she was hanging out with a young man so obviously needy like James. What was their story?

Now was not the time to find out. He followed Roger and Dale down the corridor, Alice trailing along behind him at a saunter.

They did not see any more rats.

CHAPTER TWO

Central

FROM THIRTEEN STREET TO CENTRAL TOOK about a half hour. Ethan tried, as usual, not to think too hard about the slime on the walls. At least he had gone mostly nose-numb to the smell.

They lived in these tunnels now, sharing living space with rats and the occasional sewer gator. Yes, there were actual sewer gators. The myth was real. Kinda like the zombies.

The group members walked the path automatically. They didn't have to look for the painted landmarks or the changed names. It was instinctual, like homing, allowing them to get back home even after grueling hours waiting and baking as they manned a selected kill zone and encountered a murder on what had become its turf. Dale, in one of her better moods, made jokes about how humans were actually becoming the Mole people from Mars. No matter how accurate the joke was, Ethan still could not find it in himself to laugh.

Ethan looked back, checking Alice's location. She walked, still at a somewhat slow pace, occasionally looking around. Every so often a bit of light caught her eyes and he could have sworn the colors switched sides. The green was on the left now and the hazel on the right. Shaking his head, he told himself he had gotten the sides wrong to start with.

"Don't stare," she said.

Ethan started. Alice stared straight through him, her expression a little warmer than belligerent.

"I wasn't staring." He didn't remember staring, only looking. There was a difference. When he brought up his hands, he brought up his pistol. Training dictated his reaction to a threat.

"Never point that unless you intend to shoot someone." Alice's cold tone implied she meant it. She stopped moving as if to give him a clearer shot. James hid his head behind hers because Ethan couldn't see his face at all.

Ethan lowered his gun, his motions measured.

"What the hell are y'all doing pissing around back there?" Dale's voice came from somewhere ahead in the gloom. Ethan suppressed the guilty look of fear which threatened.

"Nothing. Just a... misunderstanding." Ethan hesitated.

Alice didn't respond.

Dale said, "Stop trying to get into the weird chick's pants and hurry up."

With a sigh, Ethan holstered his gun before looking at Alice again. She smiled a not nice smile. Ethan moved to a space alone between Dale and Roger and Alice and James. It seemed safer that way.

Central was once an old subway switching station. Now, it was reinforced against intrusion and required guard access. You had to prove you weren't infected and crazy before you were allowed in. One of the reasons for the long tunnels: even if you managed to get into them after being bitten and could navigate close enough to come across a gate, by the time you made it the guard would shoot you because you'd turned. No muss, no fuss, no danger to anyone else. Once the coast was clear, someone would come out and drag the body away to be burned. No need to leave a plague body so close to the front door.

One of the leaders said they had to be ruthlessly efficient in these times. Ethan could see that in how they handled the dead.

A converted subway car served as the nearest gate to Thirteenth Street. The refugees had parked the car on the tracks where they wanted it and then carted rubble and concrete until it stood an impassable wall ten feet thick with the emergency exit door of the subway car as the only way through. The windows had been reinforced with steel so that slits remained to see through and little doors so you could point a pistol.

"Hello to the returning." The PA system rigged into the car greeted them. "Names please?"

Roger was up first. "Roger Mackie. Thirteenth Street building 2." He took off his helmet and held it under one arm.

Dale did the same. "Dale Barnard. Thirteenth Street building 4."

Ethan didn't wear a helmet. "Ethan Post. Thirteenth Street spotter."

There was some shuffling the group could hear over the PA before the person asked, "Registering one other movement signature, but no corresponding heat signature. Can you confirm?"

"Yes, we can confirm. Located a live one top side. No signs of infection." Roger spoke up. "Central has authorized entry."

"Hold position for Central confirm." The request for authorization went back to Central Command. No one was going to let someone in just because they said Central okayed it. That would just be stupid. Of course, it didn't take a whole heck of a lot of sense to do guard duty in the first place. Ethan shifted from foot to foot as the time stretched on.

"Central has confirmed, but they stated there were two. Where is the second?"

"He's here. She's carrying him." Ethan saw the eye-roll as Roger answered the question.

"Understood. Proceed through."

The door swung open, allowing one person at a time to enter and walk through. Another safety precaution: bottlenecking entrants into a kill zone in case they should make it through all the other safety precautions. It did manage to keep the body count down.

They made it through. Ethan couldn't get used to the uncomfortable feeling of being watched, by people with guns, as they hopped out the other end of the car and officially made it into Central territory.

Once they were out, Alice swung James around to the front so that he could use his arms. He was pointing at something, though not saying anything. Occasionally she would nod as if they were having what amounted to a wordless conversation.

"What's he pointing at?" Dale asked.

Alice shook her head. Apparently, whatever was going on was for her only to understand. James stopped pointing, keeping his thoughts to himself.

Central looked like what it was, a converted subway switch station. The tracks were used to push carts from one place to another. The refugees lived in converted subway cars or in hastily carved out niches in the walls. Not the lap of luxury by any means, but safe. That was enough for most. Especially when even those you loved dearly might be trying to eat your face off if you were living topside in a comfortable apartment. Besides, the electricity didn't work topside, so there was no air conditioning. At least in Central, there were working lights that didn't need batteries.

"This way." Roger waved Alice toward him. "You two can go wash up," he said to Dale and Ethan. "I'll submit the report and turn these two in."

His two companions nodded.

Ethan smiled, grateful for the chance to get a shower and try to make heads or tails out of what he had seen topside. This woman, Alice, and this man, James, who were they, what did they want, and was it liable to get anyone he knew killed? All important questions in his mind. Very important questions.

"So," Dale asked as soon as Roger started off toward what could be considered the nerve center of Central with the two pickups. "You headed for the showers or to bed or can I interest you in getting a drink before either?"

"Shower. Then maybe bed. Really don't think I can stomach a drink after all that. Did you see what she did to those zombies?"

"Yeah, got an eyeful through my scope. That kind of strength isn't human. The top of that bus is over ten feet straight up. No one can make that kind of a jump from a standing position." Dale sounded impressed.

"True." Ethan agreed. There was something weird about them. He'd been thinking that since he first picked up her running through the murder of zombies. There was no way she was normal. Even the zombies seemed to know it from the way they behaved. Ethan made the turn toward the communal showers on autopilot, his brain still picking apart every nuance of the previous encounter.

"Do you think she could be some new breed of zombie?" The question was out before he could stop it and Dale froze, looking at him with eyes the size of Grandma's dinner plates.

"Oh shit..." Her mouth dropped open and stayed that way.

Ethan waited. His thoughts zoomed in eccentric patterns as she tried to pull herself together.

"No way. They can't be organized. She's organized," Dale said.

"Forget I said anything."

"Too late. We need to let Central know."

"Central's gonna know something is up as soon as Roger gives his report and they get a good look at the both of them. You remember what the gate guard said: no heat signature. What human being doesn't produce heat?"

"Right."

Ethan started walking again, forcing Dale to follow along if she wanted to continue the conversation. She followed. Her steps hurried.

"But that would mean the virus mutated or someone's intentionally making these things. Why would anyone want to do that?" Dale asked.

"I don't know. No one really knows how they came to be in the first place. It just kinda happened and suddenly the world was going to hell in a handbasket and the zombies were the ones controlling the handlebars."

Dale didn't look amused. Ethan flushed with embarrassment.

"Sorry, mind got a bit graphic."

"Thanks for that." Sarcasm dripped off every word leading to more deep red in Ethan's face.

"So, you're sure you don't want to go talk to Central Command and let them know what you've picked up about this weird chick?"

"No. If they ask, sure, I'll say, but I'm not about to draw attention to myself. Not again," Ethan said.

Dale let it go at that.

The communal showers had the remains of thick opaque plastic tarps to keep them somewhat private. Yet Ethan still had a problem showering around Dale. Probably hormones. She wasn't unattractive. He sighed. "I'm gonna go shower."

"Yeah," she said watching the red creep further down his neck. "I know. Love to say I'd shower with you, but I know how you are."

The insinuation only made him a tomato to his ears.

"We'll talk later," she promised before taking off down the corridor at a jog.

Ethan watched her go, waiting for the gloom between the lights to swallow her up before he slipped into the shower area himself. It felt good to takeoff the gear he wore, stripping away the sweat sodden fabric and feeling the air against his skin. Eighteen hours in one area, practically terrified to go to the bathroom for fear of missing something took a toll on him. Now, he had 24 hours to himself. What was he going to do with all that time?

CHAPTER THREE

ALICE FOLLOWED ROGER AS THE GROUP split in two. James leaned his forehead against her neck; it felt cool to her skin. As they moved into more populated corridors, people stopped to look before moving on, fascinated for whatever reason. Maybe the amount of blood Alice wore. Whatever the reasoning, Alice's hackles rose at the constant eye groping.

"They're not staring at you," James offered under his breath.

"Yes, they are."

There was no real defense for this in her mind. They stared and she wanted to hurt them for it. *So tired of being stared at.* There was nothing worse.

James snuggled closer to her and shut up.

Alice fixed her eyes on Roger's back and tried not to notice the eyes crawling over her skin. If her hands hadn't been occupied, she might have tried to brush the feeling off her. With James in her arms, she couldn't. It made the need to do violence all the worse. The need to reach out and snatch the face off one of the onlookers becoming almost unbearable.

The door into the Central command was marked with a giant gold star surrounded by a red circle. Once upon a time, military commanders had worn that symbol plus a number of smaller stars around it to denote their rank. Now it was just the single interior star marking the people within as those in power. It was not impressive. Neither was the door itself. The hinges showed obvious rust. It might survive two good hits, though not more.

Roger opened the door and walked in as if he had every right to be there. The constituents of Central Command were already there, seated along a conference table.

"Roger Mackie," Roger reintroduced himself as if those at the table didn't know him. "Returning from Thirteenth Street. Presenting two found topside, unidentified. They don't appear to be infected."

Alice had found the looks in hallway uncomfortable, insects on flesh. Here the eyes were needles jammed into her skin. Again, she tamped down the need to do harm, forcing herself to look away rather than take the eye to eye contact as a form of challenge.

"What's your name?" The first question was expected, but Alice did not answer. She stared away from the group and paid them no mind.

"She's Alice," James said. "I'm James. We don't have last names. We don't know where we're from and we've been running for a long time."

The general expected questions James could answer. They probably wouldn't like the answers, but those were the ones they were going to get, like it or lump it.

"I'm sorry." A woman spoke up unconsciously smoothing her hair away from her ear. "You don't know where you came from?"

"No. Was I not clear?" James sounded confused, and it was mirrored in the cloudiness crossing his blue eye.

"Mr. Mackie," an older man interjected. "You're free to go. We'll send for you and your team for your overall report at a later time."

"Understood, sir." Roger turned to leave. He'd gone two steps before Alice was standing between him and the door with James still held securely in her arms.

"No," Alice said.

Roger looked at her with bewilderment. "What is it?"

"Don't leave."

He hesitated further, waiting to see if she was going to explain herself. When she didn't, he moved to push past her.

"Don't do that," James said. Then he looked at the group. "We're not a threat. Not now."

"What do you mean?" The same older man from before asked.

"We're not a threat now." James repeated himself as if that explained enough.

"But you could be," Roger supplied.

"This is not a game," a woman said. "You will answer our questions, or you will leave. We cannot have aliens among us who refuse to submit to our authority."

Alice turned to the woman, losing focus on Roger. The gaze she fixed on her was withering, causing uneasy shifting in not only the woman she was looking at but others on that side of the table.

For just a moment, Roger saw, clearly, a very red glitter in her eyes like a fine mist of blood.

"You have authority over us if we give it to you," James said.

Alice spoke when she wanted, but not all the time.

"Right now, we want to eat, sleep, and wash. If you want to talk to us after that, we will speak, but not be interrogated. Got it?"

ALICE

For just a moment, it seemed as if James spoke *as* Alice.

Roger had yet to hear that much force in his tone. Then James relaxed, throwing his arm around Alice's neck and settled again. She visibly relaxed as well, looking down at him instead of pinning down others with her eyes.

For a moment, a murmur went around the table before several turned to look at the lone man sitting at one end. He hadn't spoken, but he rarely did. The true leader of Central Command knew that words had power and wasting them only diminished that. There was no reason to diminish his power unnecessarily. Seconds ticked by.

"You may leave. Mr. Mackie, please escort them to the showers. I'm sure the other citizens will be more comfortable if they did not smell and look like those creatures they occasionally have to kill."

"Yes, sir, understood, sir." The relief was palpable as Roger made it to the door and Alice followed him, her behavior now placid.

As the door shut behind them, Roger heard, "We need to consider what to do with those two."

Alice stared at the now closed door. Her teeth came together with an audible click.

Without a word, Roger started walking. She would either follow him or not. Three seconds went by before he began to hear her footsteps shadowing his down the hallway.

"The showers are this way." Roger led the way. As they walked, he asked, "How did you get here?"

"Mostly on foot," James replied. "Alice can carry me for a long time, but the terrain isn't always the best, so if we can, we get a vehicle of some sort."

Meanwhile, Alice paid attention to nothing, following along with a drone's precision.

One shower ran in the communal area. When Roger stopped at the door, Alice stopped with him, looking over his shoulder and past him at the opaque plastic curtain.

"Men only beyond here, Alice," Roger said when she didn't put James down and let him walk. It wasn't actually a rule, but Roger wanted a moment alone with each of them.

Alice looked at him with a confused expression, one eyebrow going up as if to ask what exactly he meant by that. Two long seconds passed and then she looked down at James who shrugged before she put him down on the floor. He started to commando crawl using his forearms into the shower area.

"You can't walk?" Roger's tone showed his surprise.

"No," James said." Alice-- carries me--because-- it's necessary--." He continued to crawl as he spoke, making his sentence sound choppy as he seemed to hold his breath for every pull forward.

"Shit, I'm sorry." Roger scrambled forward and grabbed James under his armpits to pull him up. "Let me help you."

For someone so skinny, James was heavy. Roger grunted with the work of pulling him almost upright until Alice reached past him and bodily lifted James by the back of his shirt and settled him against Roger. It looked as if Roger supported a James who had drunk a bit too much and could not keep his feet. "Thanks Alice."

Walking forward, the intention was to leave Alice behind, but Roger stopped and turned back. "If you wait here, I'll grab whoever's in the shower out and then you and James can have it for yourselves."

He waited until Alice settled herself near the entrance before going further into the shower area. There was a chair for the older fellas to sit on while they showered, and he maneuvered it with his feet before settling James on it.

"Do you want help undressing or can you manage?"

"You'll have to do the bottom half." For the first time, James blushed, ducking his head as if to hide. "Usually Alice helps me, but yeah..." he trailed off letting the thought go.

"Gonna ask. Don't answer if you don't want to, is Alice your girlfriend?"

"Maybe. I don't really know. I just remember waking up with her standing over me and thinking I'd died and gone to heaven finally. I'm not really sure why I thought 'finally' but I remember that thought clear as day. She had a chain hanging off her neck, with a wire charm that said 'Alice'. I've been calling her that ever since."

Roger untied and pulled off each of James's shoes while he listened. Then he rolled off his socks. Obviously, the young man's clothes hadn't been changed in days. They were caked with dirt, sweat, and what Roger figured was probably blood.

"How long has she been carrying you?"

"Six months or so, I guess. It takes a lot longer to get from place to place these days. We've been walking pretty steadily, but I caught a fever two months ago and we had to stop for a while. I was worried she was going to leave me. We're going somewhere, but..." James trailed off again, the words dying in the air between them. He pulled his t-shirt over his head and dropped it on the floor.

"But?" Roger finally prompted.

It took some effort from the both of them to get James's pants and underwear off, but once they did, all Roger could do was try not to stare. James was covered in scars as if someone had simply taken a razorblade and started drawing on his skin. Some of the scars made designs; however, most were just crisscrossing single lines. They ran up and down his arms, legs, and torso, but abruptly stopped at his collar bone. It was as if the artist had not wanted to mar him for a bust of his shoulders and head.

"I don't know," James finished, looking decidedly uncomfortable under Roger's eyes. "I just want a shower. I'm tired of smelling like week old death. Could you just leave the soap next to the chair and turn the water on?"

Whatever rapport they'd built was gone. James clearly wanted him out. Roger knew how to take a hint.

"Sure." He put the soap down next to the chair and turned the water on to something close to hot. He was not going to try and scald the poor guy since he couldn't get out of the way if it got too warm for him.

"Thank you." The words were faint, but they followed Roger out of the land of tile as he went to find something that might possibly fit. Not to mention a place to burn the stuff James had been wearing. There was no way he was going to wear any of it ever again.

As Roger came out of the showers, Dale came down the corridor with a plastic cup in her hand. He didn't have to smell it to know what it was. With a grimace, he pushed the thought away. Dale wasn't his daughter. He didn't have to say anything to her about her drinking habits. She wasn't exactly alone in coping that way.

"Have you seen Alice?" Roger asked. She had been right outside the door when he went in. Now, the woman was gone.

"I thought I saw her go toward the bathroom." The showers and the bathroom stalls were nearby, but not so close one could see one from the other. Dale took a sip from her drink and offered it to the Roger. "Want some?"

"No, thank you." He declined, just as he always did. "I was just going to find them some clothes because from the looks of their wardrobe, they need it."

Dale nodded but didn't make any move to help. "Roger, Ethan said something you should hear," she whispered. "He was saying they might be some kind of new breed of zombie."

"That's not possible," Roger said. He didn't elaborate, simply putting the idea out of his mind. However, Dale persisted.

"What if they are? You saw how the murder reacted to her."

"I saw a group of zombies trying to eat someone."

"Someone who ripped several of them limb from limb."

Dale's earnestness got Roger's attention. He needed to pay attention to what she was saying, something in his gut said. There was something strange about what was going on, but he couldn't put his finger on it.

"Where is Ethan?" Roger asked. The creeping awareness of knowing grabbed him. He looked back toward the communal shower area.

"He's in the shower," Dale said indicating the shower stalls with her cup. "You said we should go wash up and get to bed." Dale had not done either of those things as yet, but then again, she needed to get a drink. Roger once again brought himself back to the thought Dale was not his daughter.

"I'm gonna go grab Ethan," Roger said. If they were something to be worried about, he didn't want anyone from his team getting killed on his watch.

Roger thrust the bundle of dirty clothes at Dale as he turned to go back the way he'd come. Whether or not James was a threat, he didn't really know, but he also didn't feel like now was a good time to trust the young man he had only just met and thus didn't really know.

Dale dropped the cup and looked down at the ball of dirty clothes in her hands before dropping them in the corridor, letting them land in the remains of her drink. Wiping her hands together, she headed toward the dressing area to scrounge up some clothes. Having some idea of what to do was better than standing there thinking about how sure she was those two were going to be the death of someone close to her.

The shower was still running over James when Roger tiptoed back into the shower area. The younger man was half asleep under the water, his dark hair wet and soapy. He looked like he was sorely in need of a nap. Since he was not blocking the drain and thus running a chance of drowning, Roger let him be and moved further back. A quick scan of the ceiling told him which showers were actually on. There was only one other in the back corner.

"Ethan?" Roger hissed as he got closer.

"Huh." The answer from inside the shower stall was confused, then Ethan poked his head out, eyes covered in soap. "Wha..."

"Nothing. It's just me." Roger felt a touch of color coming to his cheeks as he began to feel sheepish over his fears. James was no danger, no reason for Roger's heart to be beating a mile a minute.

"Hey?" James yelled for attention. "Help? Please?" The word *please* sounded as if a child said it. "Alice?" The sound of James floundering under the water was followed by a crash as he overturned the chair. "Alice!"

"James, it's okay. It's me, Roger, remember?" When he came around the corner, James was only just beginning to crawl out from under the shower curtain and into the walkway.

"Where's Alice?" James grabbed Roger's pants leg and started to pull himself up.

"She's nearby," Roger said. "Let's get you dried and in some new clothes, okay?" Whether or not James was actually clean, Roger had no intention of checking. James fallen asleep and now seemed so much out of sorts that subjecting him to any further intrusion seemed a terrible idea. Besides, he didn't know if Alice had been able to hear James calling and was thus starting to see red again.

"Hey, Ethan, you done?" Roger called. He was starting to feel rather like a den mother with all this going on.

"Yes."

"Go find out what happened to Dale and the clothes, would you?" Roger helped James back into the chair when he felt Ethan rush past him and out into the corridor.

"Where's Alice?" James asked the question again, broken fingernails dragging along the sleeves of Roger's shirt leaving behind wet trails.

"We'll get to her soon." He took a deep breath to steady his own nerves. "Soon, James, I promise, but first let's work with getting a towel around you okay?"

Roger had a twinge of pain as he remembered dealing with his own son, Robert, in a very similar manner. Granted, Robert had been five years old and James couldn't be less than 21, but the behaviors were so strikingly similar he had to stop and remember they were not the same thing or dealing with the same person.

James's eyes, mismatched brown and blue, stared unfocused as though he saw nothing at all. Roger settled him into the shower chair again and tousled his hair with a towel.

"Just be calm, okay? Ethan's gone to find Dale who has the clothes and then we'll get you dressed."

"Alice?" James's voice still held a child-like quality as he asked for his companion again.

"James, just be calm."

"Let me have him." Alice had come in without making any noise at all, wearing the remains of someone's button down dress shirt and a pair of Bermuda shorts. She looked skinny, unkempt, and maybe a little childish with her hair hanging in dark ropes down her shoulders and arms. She took the towel and tossed it over her shoulder before getting down on her knees next to the chair.

"James." For the first time, she sounded normal. "James, wake up."

"Alice." He groped forward and grabbed hold of her hair. "Don't leave me."

"Wake up, James, you're sleeping again. Nightmare's over." Alice guided his head to her shoulder where the towel was. Roger watched how tenderly she stroked James's face.

"Nightmare?" James rubbed his eyes.

"Yes, nightmare. Wake up so you can get dressed and we can eat."

James laid his head against her shoulder and finally closed his eyes. His body relaxed as though he had gone to sleep, then he opened them again and his eyes were clear.

"Alice."

"Gotta get dressed. I think food's next." She didn't mention the nightmare he'd apparently been having, but simply stood up, dragging him bodily with her. "Help me get him dressed."

Roger moved immediately, despite Alice's tone of

commanding rather than asking. For the first time, she seemed human. It helped she wasn't covered in gore.

"I always feel like I'm a toddler when you've got to pull my britches up all the time," James said.

"Well, if I didn't pull them up, you'd have to go without. Not a pretty picture."

Roger caught Alice's smile out the edge of his eye. Yes, she truly did look human as she treated James like her little brother. Maybe there was nothing more than a friendship there.

Once James's pants were pulled up, she switched to holding him by the waist and let him slip his shirt over his own head. It took two tries since he tried to include Alice in the first attempt, but once he had it on and straightened, James looked normal too. It was almost surreal when Roger considered it against the first time he saw them, her running through the murder with James in her arms, both of them covered in the previous encounters' blood, dirt, and sweat. Now she looked normal, her hair dripping slightly and holding her closest friend in a loose hug.

"So, what's for lunch?" James cracked a smile as he asked. Alice hefted him into a princess carry and shook her head, rolling her eyes.

"Whatever we've been able to scrounge," Roger offered. There was no telling what might be for dinner. One rather enterprising gentleman had decided it would be a great idea to try out fried rat. That particular entrée only lasted for one meal. The hue and cry had been epic.

"Lead the way, garcon." James said.

"I think I liked you better when you were doing less talking," Roger offered with a not so genuine smile.

"I've been living with him for six months. This is only the tip of the iceberg on his sense of humor," Alice said.

She followed along as Roger led the way back out. Dale and Ethan were waiting outside. Dale stood up against the wall while Ethan nervously shifted from foot to foot as if he were waiting to hear the results of some academic test.

"Everything okay?" Ethan asked.

"Yes," James answered.

Alice had lapsed into her silence, but her energy said *weary* more than *wary* to Roger now.

"So, food? And anyone know who is bunking where?" Dale had gotten her wind back and she took on her own quirked smile.

"I don't think the bunking issue has come up yet. Central hasn't finished talking to them." Roger shifted to take in Alice, certain of what he would find in her gaze: hate.

Alice's demeanor hardened at once.

James, in her arms, pressed his forehead to her neck and Alice relaxed.

"Mess is this way," Ethan said.

Roger shook his head and headed back in the direction of the shower. Ethan could take care of things from there.

CHAPTER FOUR

THE MESS HAD ONCE BEEN JUST AN OLD subway tunnel. Now it was closed off at one end and, somehow, they'd rigged an old restaurant stovetop to work along one wall. The counters were scrounged, along with the food, the flatware, cups, and plates. The mismatchedness which might have been quaint in small doses was just one more reminder of how much the world had gone to hell when one looked across an entire cafeteria and realized not one plate matched a single cup. Depressing was a good word to describe it. Rather like the streets above full of empty cars with broken windows, blood smears, and rotten debris.

"Alice, you and James have a seat over there. Me and Dale will work out the food situation," Ethan offered. Neither of the newcomers.

Alice settled James in a sturdy chair next to a wobbly table and then sat down next to him before kicking the chair back on two legs. She was close enough to the wall to lean on it for balance and it gave her a good view of the entire mess. James attempted to start a conversation with one or two words, but Alice ignored him the first time then waved him to shut up when he tried again. He did, a sullen pout distorting his face.

ALICE

Alice closed her eyes and listened to the movements going on around them. There were people everywhere and despite having her eyes shut, she could feel them as they tried not to pay attention to the two of them.

"We need to be ready to move on," Alice noted aloud.

"I know." James agreed nodding. "But where are we going?"

"East, here isn't it." Then she shook her head, cutting off further conversation. She opened her eyes.

Ethan and Dale joined them. Each of them carrying two plates and two cups. The food was sparse, but it was better than what one would find topside in the streets.

The group ate in silence and even Roger's return, his longish salt and pepper hair still wet from the shower, didn't spark up conversation. He simply sat down, his plate in front of him, and began to eat. Ethan finished first, having bolted his food. Dale was still pushing hers back and forth on her plate when Roger finished.

"Not finding it to your liking, Kitten?" Roger asked.

Dale took a swat at Roger for calling her that. He only chuckled and dodged away.

"Can I have it?" James eyed the greens on Dale's plate.

"Knock yourself out." She pushed the plate at him and watched him as he wolfed it all down with barely a pause for breath.

"When's the last time you ate?" Dale asked.

"Two days ago." Alice answered since James only looked up, his cheeks stuffed like a chipmunk and tried to swallow which led to a little bit of chest thumping before he could even breathe.

"Both of you?" Dale's eyebrows went up.

"Yeah. Can't eat what you don't have." The tepid water smelled slightly, but Alice sipped it anyway, carefully avoiding upsetting her stomach. "We've been moving pretty steadily, scrounging as we go."

"Where are you going?" The question was the one all three of the fighters wanted to ask. All three of them waited for the answer.

"East." Alice shrugged. "It's not here."

"If you don't know where you're going, how do you know it's not here?" Dale blurted out.

"Don't know that either. But the pulling is still there, so I'm going to take a wild guess and say it's not." Alice seemed comfortable with her lack of understanding, picking up her cup and continuing to drink it to the bottom.

"I'm going to say that sounds awfully odd," Dale said.

"Odder than a bunch of people-eating zombies roaming across the blacktop of a once great city like a new breed of buffalo?" James looked from Roger to Dale and finally Ethan waiting to see what any of them would say to that. After the initial ten seconds of silence, he went back to his plate. He stared mournfully at the emptiness as if he could will there to be more food on it.

"Point taken." Roger had to concede nothing could be stranger than that really. "What are you going to do then?"

"Eat and run." Alice looked up from her companions toa man standing over Roger's shoulder. He had not made his presence known though he'd been there since James's comment about zombies being like buffalo. He was one of those from the Central Council. The others followed Alice's look as she took him in and then gestured from him to sit down as if it were her table and he was only allowed to be there at her indulgence.

"I could not help overhearing that you won't be staying with us," the councilman said.

"You're not surprised and actually more than a little relieved. The Council wants us gone. Now," Alice said.

He swallowed hard before speaking. "Yes."

"Fine. Was there anything else?" Alice asked.

"If you return, you'll be shot on sight," the councilman said.

"Also fine. Good-bye."

Even James stopped and stared, eyes wide throughout the exchange.

"Hold on!" Ethan was on his feet before the man was up from the table. "That's not right."

"Let it go, Ethan." James tugged at the edge of Ethan's shirt. "This isn't unusual. Though the shot on sight part is new." James looked from Ethan to Alice, waiting for some indication of her feelings. She sat there with her arms crossed.

"People throw you out all the time?" Ethan asked.

"Every group we've ever come across has," James admitted with a shrug. "So yeah, not new."

"We're okay on our own." Alice put in two cents and then went back to her silence. The man from the council disappeared into the corridors of Central unchallenged and Ethan sagged back into his seat.

"This isn't right," Ethan said.

"They're taking care of their own. We're outsiders," James explained. "Besides, they want answers. We don't have any, and this isn't where we're trying to go. We weren't staying anyway."

Now that he'd lost his sense of shock, James seemed to be perfectly okay with the idea they were going to be kicked out and left to deal with whatever came. "At least we can get some decent food for the first time in days and don't have to sleep in shifts for the first time in weeks. I'd count it a good day." There was that sense of humor again, poking out from underneath all the darkness.

"I guess you're right." Ethan admitted James had a point, or three, in his take on the situation.

"In this day and age, every life but your own is disposable." Alice didn't appear to be talking to any of them, but she'd dragged a chain out from under her shirt and was toying with it. The name 'Alice' was twisted out of gold wire hanging off the gold chain.

"That's pretty," Roger offered trying to draw her back into the conversation. "Do you remember how you got it?"

"No. Just always had it, I suppose." She let the chain drop back to her chest.

"Where did you and James meet?" Roger asked.

Alice eyed him suspiciously at the question and shook her head. "Don't want to talk about it."

"Why?"

"Do you tell your life story to strangers?" she snapped.

"Alice." James put one hand on Alice's leg under the table, leaning toward her. "They aren't enemies."

"No, but they are nosy."

"No," Roger disagreed. "I just want to understand. You've been walking for six months on a feeling. You don't know where you're going, but it's okay that other people shun you."

Alice's frown deepened as she shot James a nasty look.

"It's not a big deal." James looked away, avoiding eye contact.

"I just want to understand this. You're the first people we've seen in months. The first ones and now you're leaving. We know as much about you as we did when you first appeared."

"More. You have our names," Alice countered.

"So, we do, but that tells us almost nothing. What's the world like beyond the streets we get to? Is there anything left out there to save? Are all people living like rats?"

"Why would we know anything about all people?" Alice's fists shook the table as she slammed them down and then got to her feet. There was a distinct sound of one of the table legs splintering. "We're two people, walking, that no one seems to want. What difference does it make what we know?"

"Hey Rog," Ethan put his hand on the older man's arm, pulling him to the side. "Look around."

Everyone in the room was watching the group, frozen in place as if they were nothing more than an exhibit in a museum.

"What's going on?" Roger asked.

"I don't know," Ethan said.

Alice stood, but she'd gone quiet. Every line in her body said she held her thoughts on a short lead. James had put his head down on the table and covered it with his arms. Dale looked around for what could have caused this kind of weird reaction.

Then the siren sounded.

"Breach! Breach! Breach!" The alarm system notified, and the diorama of people moved fast.

Dropped plates shattered. The staccato beat of hundreds of running feet echoed off the corridors. Everyone scrambled for weapons. If there really was a breach of Central, they were going to need every bullet in order to survive.

"Breach! Breach! Breach!" The alarm blared as Dale led the sprint in the direction of the showers. There was a good chance their gear had not been cycled through for a new group. They had guns already loaded with ammunition.

The first zombie slipped through the gate holding what was left of one of the guards in its pallid grip.

"How the fuck did those things get all the way down here?" Ethan asked as he ran in his house slippers.

"We'll figure that out later, if we're still alive." Roger shouted.

CHAPTER FIVE

BACK IN THE SHOWER AREA, DALE AND
Ethan dug frantically for their guns. Alice calmly put James on the floor.

"Stay with them," she said.

"What if you don't come back?" James asked.

"Then you're zombie chow. What difference will it make? We'll both be zombie chow." She smiled.

James didn't.

"Not funny," he said.

"Wasn't meant to be."

He sulked and crawled further into the shower area out of sight. Alice left him there, heading away from the pair looking for weapons.

"Where the hell is she going?" Dale spared a moment to look at Alice's disappearing form.

"Buying us some time." Roger joined in the search for a viable weapon. "I hope." As much as he wanted to look and see where she had truly gone, he didn't look up. Finding a gun was much more important.

The first one was a herald, a spotter, the forerunner of the invasion. Alice knew that well. Where there was one, there would be, very soon, more. However, experience had also taught her getting rid of the first one could actually

ALICE

slow down the progress. The creature now running in her direction, fangs bared, drug the entrails of its previous victim like a child with forgotten party streamers. The ends flapped and fluttered splattering blood and fluids as it came.

It was a head to head lasting only seconds.

It sprinted forward. Alice snatched its lower jaw and wrenched in one direction so hard the neck snapped. The creature spun with her momentum and when she let go, spun a little more before landing like a ragdoll its limbs all askew. The head still attempted to wiggle on its broken neck, but the arms and legs wouldn't respond to the fevered brain's entreaty to keep going. She stepped over it and headed the gate.

Alice had changed. The whites of her eyes glittered with a hellish redness and her lips curled into the kind of demonic grin often depicted on creatures from the pits. Her right hand was covered in black clotted blood, yet her nails practically glowed white underneath. Another moan came from beyond the edge of the subway car gate. The rest of the murder was coming.

The siren was still hollering about a breach as Alice stepped into the subway car and looked as the first follower stepped in through the other end. One could almost imagine the zombie recognized its end staring down the thin metal tube. However, that was giving the poor beast far too much credit. Diving forward, Alice curled into a tumble and kicked upward between its attempted grab connecting squarely with the bottom of its jaw and driving it upward with the satisfying crunch of crushing bone. The body flew backward, half landing on the one behind it. The subway car was so small the creatures had no room to spread out, leaving the more mobile Alice with a distinct advantage. One she used as she waded in again.

Meanwhile, time ticked by. The group had their weapons, but now they waited to see what would happen. Alice didn't return. Central Command had not shut off the siren, yet no one moved to do anything other than draw sightlines on the gates. Only one had been breached. The one where Alice and James had entered the supposed safe haven.

"Should we go after her?" Roger looked toward where James hid.

"Only if you leave me a gun," replied James sticking his head around the corner enough to be seen. "I don't think any of you can carry me in combat."

"He's got a point, but I don't like leaving him." Ethan pointed out the obvious flaw in them splitting up further. "If there's a problem, he'd be on his own."

"I know how to commit suicide, you know," James said.

"Let's see if we can manage to avoid that!" Ethan snapped.

James almost looked sheepish for a moment against Ethan's displeasure at his apparent final plan. With a slow movement, he crawled back behind the wall, hiding.

"So, are we going to give him a gun?" Ethan asked.

"You trust him not to shoot himself?" Roger said.

"I don't know." Dale shrugged, looking at the spot where James had been. "I don't think he'd do it."

"Probably not. Alice might decide to bring him back from the dead or something," Ethan said.

A nervous chuckle skipped around the group, even James joined in from out of sight. Roger knelt down and slid a pistol across the tiles to stop near the wall. "Don't do anything stupid with that, James. We're going to go give Alice some back up."

The three left James, bringing their guns to the ready and half-shuffling. They didn't expect to be surprised, but they weren't about to take any chances. One bite was all it took to turn an otherwise rational person into a ravenous monster. No way they were going to take that chance at all.

Roger was on point, Dale and Ethan flanking, each of them covering a wedge of space before them. They heard the sound of battle taking place, but there was no gunfire. Alice had to be on her own. Otherwise, someone would have been shooting. The strange woman apparently didn't need weapons. Then the sounds of fighting died down, as if someone had turned off a tape recorder. The siren continued to scream about a breach, but the sounds once echoing from the subway car were now gone.

"Alice, you in there?" asked Roger.

"Yeah, come on in. Party's over. Watch your step, one of them down there still has his teeth," Alice said.

When they entered the subway car, Alice was sitting on one of the benches, her legs crossed and up on the back of the chair in front of her. Clotted black blood slid down the walls and occasionally a body part on the floor twitched making the floor appear alive.

"Where's James?"

Roger blinked hard at Alice's face. "Alice, what the hell happened to you?"

"Don't know. Don't care." Her disinterest carried not only in her voice, but in the way she rose from the bench, putting one foot on the floor then the other. It was odd how each of them made sure to lower the muzzle of their guns in order to avoid the chance she might take their behavior as some kind of attack.

Then she headed for the door, waiting only long enough for them to get out of her way before she got out of the subway car.

The sound of a shot slashed the air and made the three of them start. Dale fired off a shot of her own in her nervousness.

"What the hell?" All three of them turned for the exit, Roger shouldering his way into the lead. He stopped in the doorway. Ethan craned his neck to see around him.

Alice stood just off the edge of the subway car, a half circle of men with guns 20 feet away. Two of them had James by either arm, holding him up so that his legs dragged the floor. He hung limp.

"James!" Her voice carried across the distance and her companion moved his head as if to take her in more closely.

"Alice?" Her name was a question on his lips. The motion of James's head seemed lost.

"It's going to be okay, James." There were a dozen guns trained on her and she was telling him it would be okay. "It is all going to be okay."

Alice took a step forward.

"Stop where you are, or you will be shot!" The directive was shouted by one person, but they all either cocked their guns or made it clear they would shoot at the first opportunity.

Alice stopped, her mouth dropping into a frown. A moment later, she showed her teeth.

"Give me my friend and let us leave." Though she didn't move, there was no mistaking her intention. If they wouldn't give her James, she would take him and all of their lives as well.

ALICE

Roger stepped out a little further, his own weapon still down. Ethan didn't share his sentiment, when he came out of the subway car, Ethan's weapon was up.

"Let him go!" Ethan yelled.

The look Roger shot him was half-surprise, half-unhappiness, but he didn't tell Ethan to stop or say anything when Dale did the same bringing her weapon to her shoulder. Reluctantly, he joined them, the three aiming past Alice's body at the ring of soldiers.

"Thirteenth Street Team, you are asked to stand down." The voice addressing them came from beyond the circle and it was the head of the Council. Each of them had heard it enough to know it, yet they wavered only a moment.

"Order respectfully declined." Roger spoke up for the three of them. "She stuck her neck out for us. We're doing the same. We want her and our friend, James, returned immediately."

"Negative. Return is impossible. She may stand down and accept the Council's judgment or be shot."

Alice huffed through her nose at the idea of someone shooting her before crossing her arms over her chest and shifting her weight to one leg as if to dare them to take the shot they were so busy saying they were going to give her.

"Give him back," she said.

James looked up at those holding him and wrenched back and forth, forcing them to almost drop him. They didn't let go, but he kept on twisting. His frantic motions went on for almost a full minute before Alice finally moved, unable to watch him struggle.

Three shots went off at the same time, two from the circle and one from Ethan whose trigger finger had reached the point of being exceptionally itching throughout the waiting game. Alice took two in the chest and dropped to her knees. The man Ethan shot dropped backwards.

"Alice!" James screamed and with a rabid movement, buried his teeth in the arm of one of his captors hard enough to draw blood. The other couldn't hold him up alone, so he dropped to the concrete and started crawling toward the fallen and bleeding body of his companion. He slipped his arm under her neck, looking into her empty eyes.

"Alice," he repeated her name.

There was no response.

The three could only stand and stare.

Alice was dead.

Roger jumped off the subway car, and shoved James back far enough to feel for a pulse in Alice's body. There was nothing. He put his ear to her mouth. No breathing sounds. James butted against him and put his own head to Alice's chest, smearing her blood all over his face. He moaned her name over again as he hugged her.

"Take them." The Council Leader ordered their capture with no change in his tone. In fact, he seemed pleased to see Alice dead. "Collect her body and dump it with the others. We will burn all of them together."

None of them had the heart to fight as they were swarmed by the fighters. Even James came without much more than a sob of pain. He was carried between two men, his hands covering his bloody face. Her name was the only word he seemed to know.

CHAPTER SIX

Prison

"THEY SHOT HER." ETHAN SHOOK HIS HEAD over and over again. "She didn't do anything."

"You saw what she looked like." Roger tried to rationalize what he had seen. In all the months he had been working for Central Command, he had never seen them do anything like this. Then again, most of that time he'd been living in a fog, trying not to think about the wife or son he'd lost to those monsters. "She looked like a monster. I would have probably shot her too if I didn't know she wasn't actually trying to hurt anyone."

James scooted across the floor and found his way under the cot hanging by chains from the wall. He continued to repeat Alice's name. It had become his mantra. It wasn't working because occasionally he would laugh unhappily and start babbling about a nursing home and a wheelchair. None of the others had managed to figure out what exactly he was talking about. Dale sat on top of the cot, looking at the bars holding them in. Her eyes were flat, not as empty as James's, but flat and unhappy.

"I hate bars," she muttered crossing her arms over her chest like a petulant child. "I really, really hate bars."

47

"So, do I," Ethan agreed. "They're going to burn her body like refuse." His indignation actually seemed to be coming off his body as he paced the floor. "We can't let them do that."

"What can we do about it?" Roger asked.

"We can go get it." Ethan stared back at the surprised looks from his teammates. "Come on, you know you've thought about it."

"They shot her for moving. Do you really think they are going to do less to you for deciding to break out of your cell and go steal a body from the pile they're going to set on fire?"

"I don't really care what they're going to do. They've already shot whatever respect I had for them. Their authority means nothing to me," Ethan said.

"What about your Dad?" Roger asked.

"I can't see my Dad being happy with me just standing by and letting people kill someone willing to stick out their neck for me. In fact, I'm pretty sure he'd be pissed if I sat back and let them burn her body without trying to do something about it."

"Well," Dale didn't sound convinced, but she was closer to convinced than Roger. "Do you really think it's possible?"

"We know where they keep the bodies until it's safe to burn them. All we have to do is find a way out of this cell." Ethan looked at Dale.

"Then we're out and weaponless, all of Central is going to be on our asses, and what do we do once we find her body? Bury her? Where?" Roger asked.

"I don't know. You understand I just can't stand by and do nothing, Roger."

"I understand just fine. I just don't think you understand what you're asking. You're asking us to stick out our necks and try not to die in spite of the fact that she's dead. Get it through your head: Alice is dead. There is nothing we can do about that. Why would you want to throw your life away for a dead body?" Roger threw his hands up.

"Alice," James broke into the conversation with two cents. "Alice." He repeated again, sticking his head out from under the cot. "Alice isn't dead."

"Yes, she is, James. She's dead. She didn't have a pulse. No pulse, no heartbeat, no breath, nothing." Roger got down on the floor and tried to make him understand a little better what exactly he was up against. "I'm sorry, James, but she is."

"No. She isn't." James crawled out from under the cot and breached Roger's personal space. "Alice isn't dead. She's not dead. She's not dead." His words became more frantic as he grabbed Roger by his shirt. "She's not dead."

Roger pulled away, then grabbed James by his wrists and made him let go.

"She's not dead," James blubbered into the floor while he curled into an awkward fetal position since his hips and legs refused to work. "She's not dead. Not Alice."

Ethan got down next to him and laid one hand on his back. "I'm sorry, James, but she's gone. She didn't mean to leave you."

"She didn't leave me." He seemed to be caught in the need to stop himself from seeing the truth. "Alice would never leave me."

James refused the truth; they all saw it. How do you convince someone to see something they were in denial about? You don't. Ethan pulled away and settled himself next to Dale.

"Are we going to do this or not?" Ethan asked.

"Are we going to stick our necks out over a dead body?" Roger summarized.

"Yeah. Are we going to do this or not?"

Roger might have been considering playing it safe, but Ethan had already made up his mind. He looked from Roger to Dale for support. She met his eyes and shrugged. One way or another she didn't seem to care. If they did this, they did it. If not, then there was no reason to even keep on discussing it.

Ethan turned his attention back to Roger. If he could convince the older man, then they were in business. Except Roger was definitely not on board. James had no real say one way or another.

"Roger, we can't sit here and do nothing."

"I understand, but sticking our lives out there in order to honor someone we barely knew just for the chance to bury her? How can you think this is a good idea?"

"Do you have a better idea? Do you want to sit around here until they decide executing us is a good idea too?" Ethan leaned back against the prison wall and crossed his arms.

Twelve hours had passed since the subway car stand-off. Twelve hours of being stuck in a cell with nothing to do but review what happened and reconsider every action. Would they have shot Alice if the three of them had not drawn their weapons? Would they have shot all of them if there weren't so many witnesses? Would they shoot them now in order to make sure the story didn't get out to everyone in the compound?

Roger considered those thoughts because there was absolutely nothing else to do, other than listen to his companions talk or James moan. Getting up, Roger walked over to the bars and grabbed them hard before trying to shake them. They were solid, not even a budge when he put all his weight on them.

"How are we getting out of this cell?" Roger's question caught Ethan off guard.

"You in?"

"I don't have anything left. If you think I'm going to stand by and watch you run off and get yourselves killed, you're wrong." He didn't look at Ethan as he spoke, but he stared across the tiny hall to the hooks on the other side. They were hastily added, there to hold the keys to the three cells all lined up against one wall. Before that day, Roger couldn't remember ever hearing of anyone actually being confined to them. They were just a threat in case someone got far too rowdy. Roger never thought of himself as the kind of person who would be occupying a prison cell. He was fairly certain those others with him thought the same thing.

"Thanks, Dad." Dale's joke brought a smile to Roger's face.

"If I'm Dad," he turned around to look at them. "Then shouldn't the two of you listen to me more often?"

"Just because you get to be Dad doesn't make us little kids. Remember, we're old enough to join the military." Dale stuck her tongue out at him along with her response, which actually got a full-fledged chuckle.

"All right!" Ethan moved to the bars as well. "Now we've got to find a way out of this cell."

"Pull the pins." James had turned over so that he was staring at the ceiling from underneath the cot. "I saw it in a movie once. They pulled the pins out of the door and then simply lifted it off the hinges. I thought it was stupid, but hey, whatever works. Right?"

"Will that work?" Ethan managed not to look as surprised as he felt with James offering something useful to the conversation. It was bizarre really how quickly he went from one emotion to another. One minute he was a blubbering idiot, the next he was so calm. Eerie.

"I don't know. I guess it depends on what kind of hinges they have on the door." Moving over to the door, Roger pressed his face into the bars, trying to see what kind of bolts held the door on. "Looks like it might be possible." He stuck his hand through the bars and felt the hinges. The bolt had a rounded top with a flat edge. Carefully, he ran his fingers down to the bottom. There was nothing holding it. That confirmed his suspicions. The bolts were only held in from the top. A rush job maybe? Didn't matter. They were going to use it to their advantage. "Need something to pry with."

Everyone patted down their pockets, looking for anything they might be able to pry the bolt up with.

"Think we can lift the door itself far enough?" Dale offered as she joined the pair at the door. She was the shortest of the bunch.

"Maybe." Roger had to admit it may not work. They only had so much time. Once someone came back, they were going to have a much harder time of this. "Ethan, grab one of the cross bars. Let's see if we can even manage to lift it."

Ethan nodded and grabbed one of the cross bars, bending at the knees to put as much upward thrust as he could on it. Roger mimicked his motions.

"On three. One. Two. Three."

With a grunt the pair put their knees and backs into pulling the door upward. It moved, but not enough to full slip the door out of place.

"Shit." Ethan looked disgusted as they let it go and the door fell back into place with a clang. "We could have had it."

"We need more push. Something to give us leverage," Roger said.

Dale moved away from the door, looking up at the ceiling. "There's a water pipe up there. A rope thrown over the pipe could give us more leverage."

"How do we get the rope up there? Hell, where do we get a rope?" Ethan asked.

"We've got clothes and sheets." Dale said.

Ethan shut his mouth. The sound of footsteps interrupted them.

"Hey, you bunch," a cheery voice greeted. It held a decided nasty edge to it. "Time for breakfast."

"What's going on?" Roger asked, faking ease with the situation he didn't truly feel.

"Nothing. Council's been arguing back and forth about whether or not to shoot the lot of you and burn you with your friend or just to exile you into the city wastes where the murders can get you," the mouthpiece said.

"Sounds like a lose-lose," Roger said, his smile slipping but only a touch.

"More than likely, but hey, breakfast." The guard came all the way to door with a couple of bowls. "Oatmeal, breakfast of champions. Or in your case, the condemned."

"Ewww," Dale made an ugly face scrunching up her nose. "Any fruit?"

"Yeah, got an apple or two, but you know the fruits getting scarce. Back away from the door." As a group, they moved to the other end of the cell, letting him enter and put the bowls down, and then leave, before they moved again.

James stayed under the bed; his eyes narrowed as an upset cat.

"Thanks for being smart," the guard said.

"Thanks for feeding us."

The three tabled their conversation to keep it between them. The guard stayed with them for a few minutes before he took his leave of the group. They waited five minutes after he left before returning to their previous topic.

"Rope?" Ethan asked.

"Sheets first. We'll see if that's enough. If not, shirts next." Dale said.

The group grabbed the sheets off the two cots in the room. They were only the flat sheets certainly not enough to keep warm, but hopefully they would be enough to get a long enough rope. Tied together in a clumsy knot, they weren't quite long enough, but the addition of Ethan's volunteered shirt they had enough to get it around the door bar and up over the water pipe.

"Hey James, think you can give me a hand to step up?" Dale was too short to grab the pipe.

"Why not just hang me on it? I'm heavier." James made an ugly face as he said it. "Just don't let me come crashing down."

It took Roger and Ethan to get James a hold of their makeshift rope. Then they joined him in holding onto it.

"On three." Roger was once again in charge. "One. Two. Three."

The two of them pulled hard and the door popped off the hinges like a champagne cork. Leaving them with a whole different problem. "That thing's gonna make a lot of noise."

"Then we'd better hurry." Ethan and Roger let go, letting the door come to the floor with a clang and then fall forward into the wall.

"Ethan, you're carrying James piggyback style. Dale, you, and me are covering point. We've got maybe a minute before someone comes to see about that noise."

Ethan backed up until James could transfer from the rope to his neck. He made a strangling sound until James moved his hands.

"Sorry," James said.

"You're heavy."

"Alice never seemed to mind."

"That's because she loved you too much to mention it." Ethan started forward with a grunt. "Damn. How did she do this and run?"

James opened his mouth to say something but stopped himself at the look on Roger's face.

"Snipe later. Move out!"

CHAPTER SEVEN

THE GROUP SET OUT TOGETHER. BY THE time they'd made it down three hallways, they could all see exactly how much this wasn't going to work.

"We're going to have to find you somewhere to hide, James. Until we can manage to get what we need," Roger said.

"You can't leave me alone," James said.

"Look, stow the whine. You're too heavy to carry all over the place and we need to get equipment before we take off. Otherwise, we won't get any further than a couple of streets top side."

"But..."

"Don't make me repeat myself, James. You'll be fine."

While Roger might have entertained James's whining before, this was their lives. Protocol said there was a silent alarm going out to all of those with weapons training to be on the alert for something going on without letting non-combatants know.

They were in the storage hall for the mess. Ethan squatted down and let James slip off his back. James gave them a dirty look and then rolled over to one side of the hall. Dale covered him with a tablecloth.

"We won't be gone long," Roger assured him. "Just long enough to get a few weapons and some food."

There they left him.

Fifteen minutes later, they returned to find James fast asleep on the floor underneath his blanket. Dale pulled the tablecloth off him and then nudged him with her foot.

"Wake up," Dale said,

"Go away," James mumbled. "Sleeping."

"No duh. Wake up." Dale played along with his behavior despite knowing for certain he wasn't asleep. Sleeping people didn't respond to noise in their vicinity. Half-asleep people did though. She nudged him again. "Let's go."

"No." The sleeping man turned over to face the wall, though his hips did not move with him, leaving him in a rather odd, twisted position. "Go away."

"Get up, James. We've got to go get Alice." Roger nudged him the third time, trying to force him to wakefulness.

"Alice?" James turned back toward them and opened his mismatched eyes wide to stare up at them. "Gotta go get Alice." He turned over and started to crawl forward, directionless.

"Uh, this way." Dale stood over him and pointed back the way he was going.

"Sorry." He turned over and crawled the other direction. "Yeah."

They let him crawl for a little while, then Ethan handed his pack to Dale and bodily hefted James up off the floor.

"Too slow."

"Not funny." James showed his teeth at the nickname.

"Was to me." The group moved slowly, checking out the cross halls as they moved. So far, there didn't appear to be a concentrated search for them.

"Where's the search party?" Dale asked.

"Don't know. Something is wrong. There should have been an alarm sounded by now. I don't hear anything or anyone." Roger tilted his head to listen.

"We saw that guard less than an hour ago," Ethan said. "So, what could have happened since we saw him?"

"Don't know. Do know we need to get out of here. If we're lucky enough to get out of here without a search party, then we should just take what we can get," Roger said.

They continued through the silent halls, searching for some kind of opposition.

That was when they heard it. The low groan of a zombie. They froze.

"There was no alarm," Dale whispered.

"No, there wasn't," Roger responded to her. "I'm going to check it out. Stay here."

He gestured for them to stay put, while he went to see where the moaning originated. Roger brought his gun up to his shoulder and looked down the scope as he inched forward.

Ahead, the groaning increased. Soon another voice joined it. The heavy scent of blood hit Roger in the face even over the ground-in stink of the Central compound. He slowed his breathing and ignored it.

The two voices turned into five as he stepped forward, one slow sliding step at a time. At the corner, he put his back against the wall and looked around the corner by sticking his head out only. What he saw threatened the stability of his stomach.

Five zombies, wearing clothes he recognized as belonging to Central, were congregating at the end of the hall ahead of him. They were feasting on someone else who was dead enough to no longer scream. Whether or not there was enough of the person left for them to get up once the zombies stopped eating them, he couldn't tell. However, he was pretty certain they were going to notice him before too long. Roger slipped backward, leaving the group of zombies behind.

Getting back to the others, he held up a fist to show he'd seen what they needed to see. "At least five. All of them eating. They're people from here."

"Serious?" Ethan's voice rose and Roger signaled him to get quiet.

"Yes. Somehow one of them had to have gotten in," Roger said.

James frowned at the information, but he didn't say anything. Dale looked at James, brow furrowing with concentration.

"Something bothering you?" Dale asked.

"No." James turned to look at something quite interesting on the wall next to him and Ethan.

"James, you got something to share?" Roger peered at him.

"No."

"You know something," Roger pushed.

"I don't know." Then he paused. "I *suspect* something."

"Okay, so what do you suspect?"

"The guy I bit is the reason this started here," James whispered.

"But that would mean..." The wheels turned in Roger's head, but they turned in Ethan's a touch faster.

Ethan leapt forward whilst letting go of James leaving him to go crashing to the ground.

"You fucking carry the plague!" Ethan plastered himself against the wall whilst frantically checking his bare neck for bite marks and scrapings.

"Wait. What are you saying?" Dale was a little further back on her thinking. "You turned him into a zombie?"

"Like I said, I don't know, but I *suspect*. I've been out there for six months with Alice. You saw what Alice was like. How do I know that nothing rubbed off on me?" James rolled on his stomach and started to crawl forward. "Besides, this isn't really the time to discuss it. They are still roaming around and I'm pretty sure we all taste the same species of tasty to them."

"Why did not you say something sooner?" Dale got down on the floor despite knowing she couldn't protect herself from that position. "Especially since you knew you bit that guy?"

"I bit him because he was keeping me from getting to Alice. I just want to get back to her." He rested his head against the concrete and refused to look at her. "I just want to get back to her."

Dale rubbed his hair and then got up again. "So, what are we going to do?"

"The plan hasn't changed. We still have to get out of here." Roger shouldered his weapon and listened for moaning. It wasn't any closer than it had been, but they were going to need to get away from it soon. Like before the creatures decided they were done with what they were currently eating and decided to come looking for more food.

"So, zombies that way." Roger pointed down the hall he'd gone down. "Guess we're going to take the route out through the hydroponic garden."

"The only way out of there is through the rainwater chute."

"I know, but what other choice do we have?" Roger didn't wait for the answer. "Ethan, get him up off the floor so we can go. I don't care that you think he's a plague rat. Just get him so that we can get out of here."

Ethan eyed James with suspicion, and then looked at Roger who gave him a dispassionate flat look.

"Okay, okay." Ethan put up his hands and knelt down next to James. Only Dale saw the ugly look crossing his face and the suppressed shudder as James crawled up his back to put his arms back around his neck.

Hefting his weapon, Roger pointed Dale in the right direction.

"Take point. I'll hang back with Ethan in case we've got to start running."

Dale nodded and brought her weapon to the ready, slipping along the hallway with slow steps. Roger looked back toward where he'd seen the zombies feasting on the unsuspecting. How many more were there?

He shook his head and followed Ethan along the hallway.

Dale swept the muzzle of her weapon back and forth as they made their way down the hall. She listened for the undertone of moaning beneath the compound's recycled air. Her eyes were accustomed to the gray so much that the first sight of splashed blood along the walls stood out in neon. The sight brought her to a stop.

"Roger." Even though she knew what it was, she put her fingers into it anyway, feeling the blood come off like a grease paint onto her fingertips. "We've got a problem."

Roger slipped past Ethan to join her, looking at the splashes with a sense of disbelief. "Oh my god."

While Dale would have normally made a joke or comment about how God was the last thing on anyone's mind, she stayed silent. Her mouth was a thin line, practically colorless.

"Central's screwed, isn't it?"

Dale's question only made him nod. Ethan joined them, but he added nothing to the conversation, just stared at the mess.

"Where are the bodies?" James's question only made the group go paler because they all knew exactly where the bodies were. The bodies were roaming around with their teeth showing, trying to find others to eat.

"Let's keep moving." Roger gestured to the others. "Ethan, how you feeling?"

"Like a horse." There was no amusement in his voice, and he repositioned James just to make the point. "Hey James, can I ask a question?"

"You can ask, sure." The guy had his head resting as best he could against his arm. "What is it?"

"How come you're not biting everybody and groaning like you're having bad sex all the time?" Ethan grimaced.

"Can't answer that one. Sorry." James shook his head no.

Roger listened, but he was not surprised James had no answers. The guy seemed to have no answers for anything.

"I'm only guessing it was my biting the guy that did this. I can't say for certain, so it may just be a bad coincidence," James admitted.

"Coincidence, huh?" Ethan shook his head.

About two hallways down, Dale waved them to a stop.

"Got at least one around the corner, in our way," she whispered to Roger as he joined her.

"Shit," he muttered. "We don't have a choice. There is no way we're going to get to one of the other gates. We're going to have to find a way through."

Ethan pulled to a stop next to them, leaning against the wall as best he could despite the awkwardness of holding up another person.

"What works as a zombie lure?" Ethan asked.

"People," Roger said.

"Yeah, I'd rather not be a worm, thanks much." Dale said, her dry humor poking through.

"I know, but that's what works. They come to the kill zones because they smell a live person. Why do you think the spotter is always close if not on ground level? It is what makes them come. So, we've got to find a way to simulate the effect," Roger explained.

"James, you wanna volunteer?" Ethan asked.

The disabled man gave the group the finger in response to the question.

"Okay, so that's out. Is there any other way around this area to get to the garden?" Roger opened the question to the group, listening as he did so, in hopes the moaning would not get any closer. He kept his voice down to a stage whisper.

"There's a maintenance shaft running along the top of the hallway. It's there for servicing the ventilation, but it's seriously narrow. Like can't crawl through it with a pack narrow," Dale offered. "We'll have to leave the packs or find a way to drag them through."

The moaning changed tone and shifted to their direction.

"How close is the tunnel entrance?" Roger kept his voice lower than the sounds around them, hoping not to draw any more attention to them.

"We're going to have to step out into the hallway and go that way." Dale pointed to the left, which was away from the moaning, but would make them fully visible to anyone looking straight down the hallway. "Halfway down there's a ladder built into the wall which leads up into the shaft."

"You know this because they made you go up there, didn't they?" Roger asked.

"Yeah. I don't know if Ethan will even fit, too much shoulder."

"You can't leave me here," Ethan whispered.

"Don't plan on it. But you know what? We don't have too many options here, you know?"

"I know," Ethan said, defeated.

"We're not leaving anyone behind. We've just got to find another way into the garden so we can get out of here. Otherwise, we're all screwed. Here's what we're going to do," Roger said. "We're going to drop back, fortify a position, and Dale, you're going to run through the tunnel, check the layout and where the zombies are. Then, get back to us as fast as you can. We're going to find a way out of here."

"Are you sure? The longer we stay down here, the longer we have to deal with the fact they might actually find us," Ethan said.

Roger shot Ethan a nasty look.

"I'm sure. Let's back up." Roger stood up.

"Best place, and no I'm not being funny, the refrigeration in the kitchen area. It's got a metal door and only opens out." James's suggestion got him some funny looks, but after a moment's consideration, Roger had to admit the fridge was a good idea.

"Either of you know how long it will take for a person to freeze to death sticking around in a fridge?" Roger asked the question they were all probably thinking.

"An old television show did a segment on that once." Ethan tried to remember what exactly they had said about humans being stuck in freezers for long periods.

"Yeah, I saw a show that did one too," Dale said. "I think the time limit is like 4 hours."

"If you're not back in an hour, we're going to assume something ate you and come up with a new plan," Roger said.

"Thanks. Really thanks, Roger, ye of little faith."

"Dale, stow the attitude. Ethan, let's go." Roger gestured for her to hurry.

The moaning grew louder.

"Here, take this." Dale threw her pack and her weapon in Roger's direction. "There's no way I can take them through there. Bad enough trying to squeeze me through those holes."

The extra weight only slowed Roger down a little as he and Ethan backtracked to the kitchen area. All they had to do was stay away from the sound of zombies. Thank goodness those things never learned to be silent. Everywhere they went, they groaned making their presence known.

CHAPTER EIGHT

DALE WATCHED THE TWO OF THEM AS THEY went back down the hallway, marking the flickering of the fluorescent light over their head. Then she turned the way she was going, getting down on the floor to look around the corner without coming face to face with some snarling, blood-thirsty creature. The moaning was close, but not close enough. She could manage a straight sprint to out-distance anything on that hallway. Turning her head, she searched the direction. The sudden loss of the lights drew a gasp. Dale could make out the ladder, an emergency light right next to it casting it in a deep red glow.

Every light in the compound died as though someone had flipped the switch. Ethan stopped in shock while Roger fumbled with his weapon to get it up to the ready. The addition of Dale's weapon and pack slowed him down, but he refused to drop the extra weight, fully convinced they were going to need it before the end of the day.

"Hurry up," Roger hissed at Ethan starting forward again.

They were in deep trouble. While the moaning would tell them something was near, there was no way of telling exactly where they were. Darkness had a habit of amplifying sound and distorting it. Not exactly the best thing when it came to trying to find a creature with a shambling gait and constant groan, but no other truly identifying behavior. "We need to get set up."

"Yeah." Ethan agreed and shook a little. "You awake up there?"

"Yes, I'm awake. I'm listening and I feel weird. I want Alice."

"Alice is dead, James. What do you want with a dead body?" Ethan replied.

Silence made up James's response to Ethan's question, but there was a sullenness to that silence they couldn't overlook.

"Why do you keep doing that to him?" Roger asked.

"It's the truth," Ethan said. "He needs to face it."

"She was his best friend, so just stop poking at the raw wound, okay?" Roger said.

"Roger, he's a grown up, not a little kid. There is nothing wrong with making him face up to reality. In fact, it's probably good for him."

"How about we not talk about me as though I'm not here and drop the damn subject?" James put his mouth next to Ethan's ear when he said it, making Ethan jump.

"Sure, man, whatever." Ethan filled his head with thoughts of Dale in a towel to kill the shiver underneath his skin.

The three made it back to the kitchen area and to the fridge without incident.

Wherever the zombies were, they had left for greener pastures. Inside of the freezer was quiet and empty. Vegetables from the hydroponic garden, some rat they had raised specifically for meat, and various other odds and ends had been thrown into the freezer.

All Roger cared about was the door. It opened outward, there was a chain on the outside, but he didn't see the zombies managing to open the door. They seemed to push forward only. The idea of backing up didn't occur. That was fine by him. A good steel door would withstand a lot of pressure. Exactly what they were banking on.

Dale pushed up on her hands and pulled her legs under her, a dead sprint would get her to the ladder before those things even truly knew she was there. Her t-shirt carried the grime and blood stains from the floor with her as she started, making one last check to insure there was nothing in her way and that her pursuit was far enough back she truly had a chance.

A scream slashed the air. Dale froze, refusing to even breathe in response to the sound. *Who was that?* The voice didn't come with a name. Fine by her, probably someone she didn't know, which meant they were on their own in her opinion. The moan of the zombies changed in tone and suddenly they were running. Dale flattened against the floor again, putting her arms over her head in hopes it would keep her from being noticed. Whether the movement did or not, the screams went from fearful to frantic as the sound of the zombies intensified. Then came the ripping and tearing, shredding flesh.

Dale could imagine the blood as it splashed across the walls. Once again, she checked her path and this time, she took off, her own footsteps echoing back off the concrete walls adding to the terror in her heart. Her fingers made contact with the ladder far too soon for her brain, but there was no time to ponder it. The running noise was now following her. She leapt up the ladder, slamming her fist into the trap door above her. It gave. Her heart skipped a beat in happiness, then she was up and shimmying through the hole. When it snapped shut behind her, she stopped with a sigh of relief.

That moment lasted for the space of two breaths and then she was commando crawling forward, the tops of the pipes over her head caressing her hair with every movement. The ventilation shaft was so small she felt like taking a deep breath would be too much. At the next trap door, she opened it and looked down into the hall below.

Dale held her breath at the sight. Three zombies crowded around the mutilated body of a woman, and from what Dale could make out, the body of a child underneath.

Both were dead.

Horrified, Dale slid the trap door shut again, crawling onward. Getting the zombies out of the hallway was going to be a bitch. If only she'd brought her gun, then she could have shot the lot of them.

Of course, shooting them would only make more of them come. Dale took small breaths and kept crawling.

A sudden open space made her stop. There was a fan above her, lazily turning to draw air into the compound. Dale looked upward, catching a glimpse of the blue sky above. Air, just a suggestion of white clouds, her heart longed for that above and the freedom it promised. Closing her eyes, she forced herself to keep going forward. Ethan and Roger waited on her. James too. Alice, well Alice would wait forever. The dead could do that.

Back in the freezer, Ethan closed his eyes, forcing himself not to think about the possibility of dying in a freezer with zombies banging on the door. It would make more sense than when that guy had been locked in by his boss, but still it would suck as a way to die. Opening his eyes, he looked at his companions. James slept, as far as Ethan could tell. Roger sat on a box of cans; eyes trained on the door. Nothing was happening, but that didn't mean it was going to stay that way.

Roger murmured, "Come on, Dale."

"She'll make it." Ethan tried to sound certain and almost made it. "How the hell can he sleep at a time like this?" Ethan jerked his thumb at James.

"I don't know," Roger replied to Ethan's question absent-mindedly. "He's strange, but then again, looking at the company he was keeping, how do we expect him to be normal?"

"You guys just love talking about me as though I don't exist and it's kind of exasperating," James said.

"Exasper-what?" Ethan frowned.

"Exasperating, annoying, bothersome, irritating," James replied.

"We're annoying?" Ethan's combative tone resounded in the small space. "You possibly make zombies, don't tell anybody, and then behave as if we should be all okay with you?"

"I don't know if that's true or not. I already told you." James levered himself up on one of boxes and looked at the two men with him. "I do know Alice was everything to me. I do know I put up a lot of shit from quote unquote normal folks just because I can't walk, and I happened to be traveling with a woman who was a sadist without a closet to hide in. Or maybe she had just abandoned it all together, leaving it somewhere in Los Angeles where we met. I don't know. I loved Alice. Alice looked out for me.

She did everything she could for me and you fuckers with your damn military bullshit took her away. And I'm the one with issues? She didn't do anything to anyone. All she did was try to protect those around her, even if they did hate her. You just don't get it. Everyone we've met since I met Alice has treated us like garbage. You guys were not the first people to take shots at us without knowing we weren't dangerous to you." There were tears appearing in his eyes and his speech became thick with emotion. "They shot her. They shot her. They shot her for no reason, and you're pissed off because I bit some guy who deserved what he fuckin' got?"

"James, calm down." Roger sounded calmer than his quivering hands said he was. "Alice's death was a tragedy, but you have to admit we are trying to survive in a situation you helped to cause with that bite."

"Fuck you, Roger." James showed a finger to both of them. "Fuck both of you. If I'm such a damn problem, leave me here. Let me die near where Alice died. You'll make better time without me."

"No because you know what, Alice stuck her neck out to protect you and we failed to look out for her, failed to help her when she did what she could to help us. She stopped an invasion and you brought us a new one. Now we have no choice but to survive and make it out of here. Otherwise, everyone is screwed."

"The whole damn world is already screwed, or did you miss the memo?" James shouted. "Zombies are eating what's left of the populace. Those who aren't dead already are living like rats in order to survive in a world so hostile there is no chance to relax."

"We know. We know, but do you really want to just

roll over and give up? Would Alice have done that?" Roger asked.

"Alice was so definitely not the kind of person who would roll over for anything," James said. "Hell, I can't think even if she were normal, she would have just stood by for a zombie attack." A smirk passed across his face then disappeared again. He rubbed his arms up and down before blowing on his hands. "This is fucking stupid. Who hides in a freezer?"

"Someone who doesn't want to be dinner," Ethan said.

"Look around, hotshot, we're surrounded by the fixings." James rubbed his hands together.

"Quit it both of you." Roger had already thrown up his hands on dealing with the two of them. "Really, we've got to survive in here. Won't do at all for Dale to get back to us and find we've hacked each other into little pieces over a bunch of bullshit."

"Dale would probably laugh and then just leave us to finish freezing."

James laughed at Ethan's assessment of their teammate. Dale might have been the smallest one of the bunch, but she made up for any deficits with enough attitude for three.

"She any good in bed?" James's question got an outright blush from Ethan, though in the darkness of the freezer, it was difficult to truly see it.

"Did you seriously just ask me that?" Ethan replied after a minute of recovery. "Is Dale any good in bed?"

"Well, I'm just assuming she's your girlfriend or something with the way she looks at you and all."

"The way she looks at me? What are you smoking and where can I get some? Dale thinks of me like her little brother."

Roger raised an eyebrow but said nothing. He'd heard the innuendo thrown back and forth between Dale and Ethan enough times to know that no girl spoke to her little brother like that, not even if she was a porn star would she be getting that fresh with a member of her family. Again, he thought about the comparative age of those around him. He was the old man of the group. It was probably going to be a long couple of days if they didn't get any other survivors.

He had a horrid thought of just walking out and letting himself be eaten by a zombie. It might be easier on his brain.

"Hey, old man," James called for his attention. "You fall asleep over there?"

"No, I'm just refusing to think about Dale in that context."

"She your daughter?" James asked.

"No. I had a son and he didn't survive the first few hours of this..." Roger let the sentence trail off into the air, unable to find a word to accurately describe the things he and those around him were dealing with now. Zombies everywhere, food scarce, life dwindling away before their eyes.

"Sorry." James managed.

Roger didn't believe he actually was, but he might be by some miracle.

"Did he go quick?"

"I shot him, so I hope so." Roger cleared his throat and started to drum absently on the carton underneath him. Anything to take his mind off of the mess they were in and the look in his little boy's eyes as the lights went out for the last time. It was one clean shot, straight through his forehead. Robert had lunged for his father's throat. Roger hadn't been prepared to die. However, he had also not been prepared to have to kill his son.

"James, what was it like traveling with Alice?" Ethan changed the subject.

"She sang a lot or at least hummed. Said it made the miles go faster."

At least he was willing to talk without throwing some kind of hissy fit.

"Alice could cook too. It was funny really, because she'd imitate things but not be able to remember exactly where she saw it the first time. I stopped asking after she started triple flipping pancakes. We were hiding out in an old Denny's restaurant and they had some pancake mix left. We had pancakes for almost a week after that. We wrapped them up and took them with us."

"Did she carry you the whole way?" Roger asked.

"Sometimes we'd manage to pick up a wheelchair or something and she'd push it or let me push myself, but mostly yeah, she carried me. Never complained about it. Said I wasn't heavy. Which is why I don't get why you think I am. You've got to be like twice Alice's muscle mass."

"Yeah, I don't know either, but I don't think I've ever stuck my hand through a person before and managed to rip out an organ. Even with their flesh being somewhat rotty. That shouldn't have happened." Ethan shrugged.

"She always fights them. I keep telling her she shouldn't do that, fighting them only means more will notice we're around, but she can't let a group of them pass by without taking them all out." James rolled forward so that he could get into a box. "I think I found some chocolate." He brought the unmarked box to his nose. "Oh, good chocolate. Anybody want some?"

"And this is probably why you're classified as heavy. Eating like a glutton," Ethan said.

"Hey, a guy's got to keep his strength up. Besides, it's not like we're leaving it for anybody if zombies have overrun the place."

ALICE

"You know what, James? You could've stopped at that first part. Next time do that. Just stop at the first part." Ethan shook his head.

"So, I should have mentioned the zombies first?" James quirked an eyebrow.

"Just shut up. Eat your chocolate and shut up."

The solid smacking sound of Ethan hitting his own face made Roger smile. They would probably have been great friends under normal circumstances, like James not being a possible plague carrier and Ethan not being a jaded survivor of the zombie apocalypse. In a nice, simple school setting where there were girls to look at and tests to cram for and scholarships to gain, they might have gotten along great. Wishful thinking since the world where that was the norm had disappeared in a flash of bloody flesh.

The candy wrapper ripping was followed by the sound of a mouth being crammed full of confection. At least it shut James up for a little while. Both Ethan and Roger could be happy with that thought.

"How long has it been?" Ethan asked.

"I'm not sure, but probably no more than a half hour," Roger said.

"So, an hour and half before we really need to start to worry."

"I think we'll have started to worry by then, in fact, I'm worrying now. Let's just say it's too early to panic."

"Panicking doesn't help anything, you know." James managed around a mouthful of chocolate. "Actually, it makes you less likely to notice the obvious and almost guarantees you're going to end up zombie fast food."

"What part off shut up and eat your chocolate did you not understand?" Ethan asked.

James smiled, his teeth stained a rich brown, and went on chewing.

CHAPTER NINE

DALE REACHED THE END OF THE VENTILATION shaft and stopped, unsure of what to do. Taking stock of what she had with her, she could only smile an unhappy smile and chuckle a sick chuckle.

"Left all my weapons. How the fuck am I going to do this?"

The walls didn't have an answer. In truth she couldn't even be sure they were listening. "Okay, Roger said find a way through. A way that doesn't involve trying to crawl Ethan's fat ass through these tunnels. So gotta clear out the zombies. How?"

For a few long moments, she considered what she was up against. Zombies weren't bright, but they were quick, and they traveled in groups. If she tried to make a run for it, she would be trying to outrun a pack of wild dogs. Even if she could manage it, where was she going to go?

"Think, Dale, think."

The hallway led to the hydro-garden. That was the only thing down there. What else came off this hall?

Lying there with her face pressed into the floor, she concentrated on remembering the layout. There were only two ways into the garden, through the hallway or the rainwater chute. The rainwater chute was a converted tunnel you could actually climb up to get to the surface. That was their exit strategy since the gates were probably all compromised.

"The shed room." The idea clicked into place with a sound she could practically hear in her own ears. The shed room wasn't a room at all, but a secondary tunnel. The far end was blasted shut so it was closed in, but there was enough space where maybe she could manage to lead the zombies in and then make it out before they got a hand on her.

That was a big maybe; a really, really big maybe. Dale took two slow deep breaths before she started to move in hopes a better idea would surface. Using herself as bait was definitely not what she wanted to do, but they had to clear that hallway in order to escape. With slow movements, she pried up the trap door and looked down into the hallway below. There were none in sight, but that didn't mean anything, since with the lights out, her visibility was down to just around the emergency lights, perhaps five feet along the hallway.

One more thing she was not looking forward to at all, running through the dark with the human equivalent of a snarling mindless dog on her heels. Dale brushed her hair back with quick fingers before swinging her body around and dropping down into the hallway. Her knees absorbed the impact and she listened for any sign someone or something might have heard her. So far, nothing. That was good enough for her. With cautious sliding steps, she moved forward, unconsciously aware of the circle of bloody light cast by the emergency lamp near the ventilation shaft's ladder.

Once she was out of its light, she zeroed in on the next one down the line, praying under her breath as she moved.

Dale had never been the religious sort, but she found her religion over again when she was forced to deal with the dead. For some reason, they made her remember her Hail Mary's very clearly.

"Mother, I miss you." Thinking of the rosary and Hail Marys always made her think of her mother, her first religious teacher. Thankfully, she passed away before the advent of the zombies. Dale couldn't even begin to imagine what it would have been like to face her mother as she knew Ethan had once faced his own mother and sister or Roger against his own son. How she would have survived looking into her mother's eyes knowing there was nothing there anymore? She didn't know. In fact, she probably wouldn't have at all.

One bullet for her mother, then another for herself. Right up through her soft palette so it would be quick and painless. If she came back as a monster, it did not matter really. None of it would have mattered.

"Watch over me and help me get out of this." Dale was nearly to the next circle of light when the first groan came. Underneath the groan came the shuffling sound of moving feet. Dale began to back up, one long stride at a time. A body appeared down the hall, coming toward her. The shadows said there were others beyond it, but she couldn't quite make out how many. It didn't really matter. The shuffling sped up as it changed into run.

Dale turned tail and gave it everything she had. Her head start shrunk as the others began to join the first in her pursuit. The tiny murder of five ran all out, their arms stretched forward, hands grasping at Dale who stayed out of reach by mere inches toward the end. She burst through the door of the tool room and was greeted by a dozen eyes staring at her.

"Oh shit!"

Two handguns. She dropped to the floor as they opened fire. Bullets ripped into the creatures following her, knocking them back into the wall. The ones behind barely noticed, they only kept running forward to be mowed down as well. Dale laid on the floor with her arms over her head and waited for the shooting to stop.

"Identify." The command echoed off the walls and then the door was slammed.

"Dale Barnard. Thirteenth Street shooter."

"She's with that group they locked up."

Dale heard the whisper passed around the group. It was rather annoying, but there was nothing she could do about it. Pressing her face further into the concrete, Dale fully expected to have a gun pressed to the back of her head and unloaded. Thus, the sense of hot steel against the nape of her neck brought her comfort.

"True?" asked the person standing over her.

"Yeah. Me, Roger, Ethan, and James are trying to find a way out of here. We think there's a way out through the rainwater chute. Figured cutting and running was in our best interest." Dale knew trying to hide her intentions wouldn't help her any real way when it came right down to it. They were either going to shoot her or they weren't. Lying and or trying to be deceptive would just likely get her shot sooner.

"James, the cripple?" The male voice asked.

"Yeah. It was his friend they shot. We don't think he deserves to die in prison. Neither do we," Dale said.

There was grumbling and mumbling over her head and she took another slow breath, thinking there had been a time when the smell coming up from the floor would have been enough to make her gag. Now she would rather smell the floor than look up into the face of the person with the gun pressed against the back of her head.

"Should we shoot her?" the male asked.

"She's a shooter. Have to be a good shot for that. We could use the extra hand. Roger too." None of the voices sounded familiar, but they seemed to know enough about the Thirteenth Street crew that Dale was unsure of what to think. It wasn't like they were famous. Why did anyone know anything about them?

"What about the other two?" asked the pistol packer.

"Don't know. We'll have to deal with that when we get to it." The touch of the pistol shifted, pressing down harder. "Where are they?"

"The freezer back in the kitchen. We were looking for a way out. I told you that."

"Okay, you're gonna take Patty with you back to the freezer, get the bunch of them out, and bring them back here. We'll all go from there," the male ordered.

Dale made a face, keeping it as hidden as she could. Now some new guy was giving her orders.

"Sure, whatever. Let me up."

The gun was removed, and Dale pushed herself up on her knees. There were faces arranged in a circle around her and she thought for just a moment they were going to dive in and start chewing.

"Patty, help her out," the leader said.

"I don't have a gun. I came through the ventilation system." Dale raised her hands over her head.

"Are there that many zombies running around?" asked a member of the group, a scrawny guy with his glasses sitting askew.

"Don't know. Maybe. Didn't want to take chances." Dale shrugged and started for the door. She wasn't going to ask them for a gun. She had one, back with her friends. Patty was two steps behind her as she reached the door. Putting her hand on the door, she put her ear against it, listening to see if something was moving around beyond it.

"Sounds clear." She opened the door. The hall beyond it was silent, empty. Dale let out a breath she didn't know she was holding as she stepped out. "Get ready to make a run for it, as quietly as you can."

As Dale ran down the hall, adrenaline pumped through her veins. While she should have been paying attention to where Patty was, Dale wasn't looking. No, she was just busy running; let Patty figure out what she wanted to do on her own. The trip back was so much shorter than the crawl out there.

"Hey." Dale banged on the freezer door while screaming at the top of her lungs. "Guys, let's go. Targets neutralized."

Inside the freezer, James perked up his ears. His two compatriots had decided a nap was a good idea, but James was wide awake. He crawled toward the freezer door before realizing there was no way he would be able to reach the latch in order to open it.

"Shit," he muttered under his breath as he crawled over to Ethan. Then he thumped his fist directly into the young man's chest. Ethan sucked in a deep breath and almost choked on it.

"Dale's back. Wake Roger." James moved toward the door again, starting to yell himself. "Cool your jets, Daley. We're coming."

Roger opened his eyes to the commotion, then rubbed them hard. He had slept harder than he'd expected, but he'd been running on fumes for a while. It was not like he'd had time to actually sleep since they'd gone on shift. He wasn't even sure what day it was anymore. The hours blended together.

"Dale." Roger got up.

"Outside the door, old man. I'm thinking we've got a problem." Ethan picked up his pistol on the way to the door. Then he hit the emergency latch, immediately bringing his gun to the ready, certain he was going to be facing more than one dead person. Dale stood there; her expression angry as it could be. Beyond her was a redhead Ethan remembered rather well.

"Patty?"

"Yeah, Ethan. It's me. Get your stuff. We're out of here. Bryan's got a bunch of people held up in the tool room. We're getting out together."

Roger pulled himself together enough to take stock of the situation. "Bryan Stride?"

Patty nodded, lowering her gun.

Bryan Stride was a member of the Central Command, one of those who had sat at the table when Alice and James were brought in. Roger was almost surprised he'd made it out alive enough to be able to pull anyone together. That meant reevaluating his assessment of the other man. Of course, there was the chance Bryan had abandoned his post in order to save those few he could.

"Ethan, get James. We're getting out of here now." The trio pulled together. Patty stood off to one side. "Lead the way."

Getting to the group went quickly. Bryan was waiting for them, his gun drawn. His group was huddled at the other end of the room.

"Let's get out of here." Roger waved at the bunch. Bryan put up one hand to stop their movement.

"Did you really start this like they think you did?" Brian asked.

"No, and I don't intend to become a victim of it if I can avoid it." Roger lied without batting an eyelash. Whether or not James was truly involved, Roger had already made the decision to protect him. Telling others, he might be the reason all of this happened was not a good way to make that happen in his book. "Get your folks together and let's get out of here."

James, wisely, kept his mouth shut.

"You're carrying the cripple?" Bryan looked incredulous as he surveyed the smaller group. "Be faster to leave him."

"My team, my choice." Roger snapped out. "Either let's go or wait here. I don't care. We're leaving."

"All right." Bryan put up his hands in a gesture of defeat. "Let's roll out."

The group headed, as one, for the door. A few wore combat gear, but most wore what passed for civilian clothes among Central.

Two minutes later, the group now grown from four to eleven, walked into the hydroponic garden, or hydro-garden as it had been called. It had once been a cistern, but the community's needs of the moved it from there to being one of the few sources of food. Scavenging had become scarce.

While ranging away from Central was possible, what did you do if you were cut off from home by a murder? It had happened a time or two. Thus, the decision was made to cut the scavenging operations in favor of killing what they could and growing food in response. The room smelled of water and greenery, far better than the underlying sewage odor that plagued the rest of Central. They'd become used to the stink so much that going out into the garden really did make it seem as if they were outside. Of course, without the overhead lights, there was just the reflected light from the high skylights above.

The rainwater chute was at the far side and the way

water came running into the cistern. It had also been the way many bodies had ended up in the deep water. It had taken a week to clean out and the stink of the burned bodies hung over Central for twice that long.

"Dale, take point. Get to the chute. Ethan, I'm dropping back to cover our retreat. You take James and follow Dale."

"Are you serious? Even with the reflected light it's near impossible to see in here," Ethan said.

"I'm serious. Just do it. Okay?" Roger glared at him.

"I can see just fine." James spoke up for the first time in a while, whispering in Ethan's ear.

"What? It's pitch black." Ethan whispered back.

"So? Ethan, just trust me. I'll guide. Stay near Dale. Everyone needs to form a human chain following you. That way Dale and Roger can shoot if necessary," James said.

"Okay. This had better not be a joke, man." Ethan shook his head.

"No joke, just go."

Ethan increased his speed, moving up in the group until he was directly behind Dale.

"Dale." She turned to look at the sound of her name. "James says he can see just fine. We're going to stay close. Don't worry."

What Dale saw when she turned around was a pair of eyes glowing in the dark like a cat's, except most cats had eyes that turned bright yellow or green in the low light. James's eyes were glittering red like Alice's had when she took on her opponents.

Slowly, Dale swallowed before going forward. The sight was burned into her memory, even as she tried not to think about it. She shifted her weapon just slightly and slid her feet along the floor to steady her footing. There was no telling when something was coming and the catwalks running just above the edge of the water were known for being slippery at the worst times.

James moved his head to either side of Ethan's as he looked at the area before them. Dale appeared as a moving shadow outlined in red and pulsating with what he guessed was her heartbeat. It was going awfully fast.

"Ethan, tell Dale to slow down. There's something ahead and I can't tell what it is." It was another shadow, vaguely humanoid in shape, but it was too big to be a person. The whisper didn't carry far, so Ethan let go with one hand to put the other on Dale's back.

"Slow up. There's something ahead." Dale stopped and dropped down on one knee. She kept her gun trained ahead. "James, got anything?"

"Don't know. It's big though. I'm surprised you can't see it." He shifted, craning forward to get a better look at it.

Then it moved. First, it was a part of the wall, far away, then it was moving forward, putting one giant foot on a catwalk. The vibration ran down the length and up through the soles of their shoes. "I don't know what it is, but it's coming this way."

As soon as he said it, the ground shook again, and the vibration took on a rhythm. It was running toward them.

"Dale, shoot it. You're aimed right, just start firing." The excitement in James's voice seemed out of place.

Dale opened fire from her knelt position. She looked like a soldier down like that, but it gave her a good shot at its knees. The first bullet did exactly that, impacted its kneecap and ricocheted. Dale just kept shooting. It was within five yards, Dale saw in the pitch black of the middle of cistern when it went down, falling off the catwalk and throwing up a wave of water.

Dale braced herself. Ethan tried to, but the wave threw him to one side, knocking James loose. James rolled and attempted to grab the catwalk and slow his movement. His hands were too slippery. He slid into the water with a much smaller splash and was face to face with the creature attempting to get back to the surface.

It had been human once. Now it was an amalgamation of parts in human shape. Its head was a mash up of skulls held together by tattered skin. It was as if a child had stitched together a face and draped it poorly over a model. The eyes were mismatched, brown and blue, like James's own. Unlike his though, they were empty, dead, and soulless. James had never truly thought he could see something like that in anything other than a monster. He automatically labeled the creature in question a monster and waved his arms up and down to get to the surface.

That was when the first bullet cut the water. Its path appeared like a plane's contrail.

"Shit!" James blew bubbles and tried to push away from the first bullet in hopes of not being hit with any that followed.

The creature was hit, but like the first bullet, it bounced off. There was nothing quite like it, except perhaps shooting directly at a steel plate. James's frantic movements got its attention. Despite the bullets, it turned toward him, its motions leaving behind a trail of blood and skin in the water. James could feel his heart *thudding* against his chest and the darkness on the edges of his vision came less and less from lack of light and more from the fact he couldn't seem to find the surface. His panic kept him from breaking the plane of water to take in air.

A hand took him by the back of his shirt and hauled him upward. The creature was not floating, but it was trying to swim despite how many times it had been shot. James gasped as his head came above the water, reflexively grabbing for the hands holding him up. Two people were holding him, one on each side.

Dale was off to one side, her gun at the ready waiting for the monster to break the surface as well. The bullets being shot into the water weren't stopping it, but it was obvious it took damage; otherwise, it would not have fallen off in the first place. She waited for the opportune moment. James saw Roger taking a knee at the other end of the group. Roger held his fire, gun forward, eyes trained on the water.

James wondered how well they were seeing at all when it came right down to it. How were they even able to take in the monster coming for them all? It didn't matter. It came out of the water with what sounded like a thousand people screaming all at once in rage and pain.

"Kill it! Kill it!" James screamed.

Dale breathed.

Roger sat like a statue.

"Kill it," James said once more.

Two shots went off. The eyes were gone. Blown-out candles in the dark. There was another splash, smaller than the first, as it sank back down into the watery depths of the cistern. James shivered, wet, and frightened. The two holding him up began to step backward, dragging him up as they did. Dale threw her arm in and the familiar smell of Ethan opened his nose.

"What was that?" Ethan asked the question on everyone's lips.

"I don't know, but it was like me." James spoke before he thought and immediately regretted it.

"Like you?" Bryan asked.

The look on his face settled him firmly in the 'I don't like you' category of James's brain. No matter how righteous his feelings might have been, there was nothing that could make James want to deal with him.

"Like you how?"

"The eyes were mismatched, like mine," James admitted, turned over, and sat. "Ethan, you gonna get me or am I dragging my own self the rest of the way?"

"I've got you." Ethan threw one arm around his shoulders and then stood up while Dale helped to get James situated on his back again.

Then, without any further orders, she readied her weapon, and started forward again. They had to get out of this place, preferably before the zombies made it down this far and started chasing them across an area they could barely see. Roger, still at the back, nodded in approval at their behavior.

"Halt."

Bryan however stood livid.

"We've got to go," Dale protested.

"We're not taking something that could become another zombie with us. Are we?" Bryan tried to stare her down, but Dale simply stared back. Ethan shifted James on his back, all too aware of the wetness invading his own clothes. They would both be shivering before too long. They needed to get out of these clothes, but now was not the time.

"Look, we're helping you to get out of here. What you do after that isn't our business. You can go back and play zombie hokey pokey for all I care, but we are not going to leave a friend just because you say we should." Dale's contentious temperament was coming out in full force. James was the only reason they had seen that thing before it got close enough to take a chunk out of someone. Leaving him behind would just be stupid.

"Dale, stand down." Roger ordered it from where he stood, then pushed to the front of the group. "Either you can come with us, or we can part company here." His calm tone held an edge that showed he had no intention of arguing.

The wheels turning in Bryan's head were obvious through his stance. He had one other good shot amongst his people. They had three, even with one of them having to carry James. Not to mention, they had the person with an ability to see in the pitch darkness the tunnels had become. It would be suicide to let them leave them standing around in the dark.

"All right, but once we're out, you and yours are gone."

"No argument." Roger agreed and then waved Dale to continue forward ahead of them. Again, Roger dropped back and took up the rear. They needed a gun back there and it kept people from being stupid and trying to go back when there was nothing back there for anyone.

"James," Ethan whispered. "You didn't just mean the eyes, did you?"

"I'm not sure, Ethan. I'm really not." James whispered to keep the conversation between the two of them. "There was something else familiar, but I can't put my finger on it."

The group moved forward into the dark and James settled his head on Ethan's shoulder, looking out for anything else that might be coming their way. He saw nothing.

The rainwater chute had been a tunnel at one point, put there for water runoff from the street above. It was wide enough to fit a full-grown human, but it was not exactly meant to be climbed. Dale looked up the length to the sliver of sky above. It wasn't dark yet, but it turned an amber hue. Sunset was approaching.

"We're gonna have to hurry this up," she called back. "Night's coming."

Various expletives followed her announcement. Roger once again moved forward from the back as they clustered around the hole. He looked up the chute as well, calculating the distance mentally.

"How long will it take you to climb it and find a tie off?" he asked.

"Can't say." Dale looked over to Roger. "It's a long way. The walls aren't exactly made for climbing, and there's no telling what the surface level looks like by now."

"Is that an *it can't be done*?"

"No, sir, just that we're walking blind into a possible clusterfuck." Dale minced no words. It had been a good plan in theory, but in practice, it left a few things to be desired, like some certainty. "Take it or leave it?"

She offered him her weapon.

"Take it. You might need it when you get to the top. Tie the rope around your waist until you get to the top, then find something sturdy to tie it off to. We'll have to make this as quick as we can."

"Or," someone offered, "we could stay here until morning."

"Do you remember that thing?" James's tone said he thought the idea was idiotic and was trying hard to hide it. Not well enough though. "Want to lay odds it has friends or family members?"

"Like you?" Whoever said it got four sets of unhappy eyes. They didn't speak up again.

Dale tied the rope securely around her waist, tight enough that it was biting into her t-shirt, and slung her weapon across her back before Roger gave her a lift to the end of the tunnel. She grabbed the nearest seam and braced her feet as best she could.

While Dale climbed the chute, the others waited. Time was against them. A half hour later, the end of the rope plopped down and coiled on the floor. At the top of the chute, Dale laid on her stomach. Roger grabbed the rope and tugged on it. The gesture she made in response might have been giving him the finger or giving him a thumbs up, it was a little hard for him to tell from that distance.

"James, you're up," Roger said.

"Wait, what?" Bryan looked at Roger as if he'd grown another head.

"He's going to take the longest because he doesn't have the use of his legs. I'm not leaving him down here to be left behind if we have to rush, so like it or lump it. I'll go up last, if that will help you feel better?"

The concession appeased the other man at least a little; though he still looked unhappy with the prospect of sending the crippled zombie maker up before those who had real possibility. Roger would have happily given him the finger without thinking about it. Probably was not a good idea, but he almost did it anyway. There was a reason he disliked that guy. This only made it more prominent. He was only in it for himself.

Roger held the rope while Ethan stood close enough for James to grab hold. Then the older man shoved a pistol in James's waistband. "You're all the backup Dale has until we get up there. Don't let me down."

"Gotcha, old man. Don't let the zombies eat the chipmunk." James grinned.

"I dare you to call Dale that to her face," Ethan said.

"I like my face, E. Why the hell would I do that?" James smiled at the both of them and started climbing. He did a hand-over-hand pull, his legs dangling beneath him. Behind him went several of Bryan's folks including Patty who gave Ethan an odd look which he returned by raising an eyebrow in question. It took almost the same amount of time to get down to just Bryan and Roger as it did for Dale to climb the chute.

"After you." Roger held the rope for the other man. "Just don't cut it before I have a chance to get to the top."

A moan sprung up out of the dark.

"Scratch that, looks like we're both going to be getting out of here double quick." Roger gestured up the rope.

The two leaders went up the rope one after the other. Then, despite knowing no zombie would ever be smart enough to climb it, they pulled the rope up and coiled it at the top of the chute.

"All right. We're out." Bryan dust himself off as he spoke. "You can take yours and go wherever. We're going to find someplace safe to stay."

"As you wish." Roger accepted his choice without argument. "We've got to find Alice. Which means finding a safe way back down into the tunnels."

"Alice?" Bryan said her name in a tone of contemplation. "She was the one they shot?"

"Yeah."

"Free advice. Her body was thrown out with the garbage. You don't have to go all the way down to get to her. Just to the burn area near the Kingston Road exit. They were planning on setting a fire there, but I don't know if they ever got around to it. Things went bad awfully quick."

With a quick scan, Roger looked for street signs to see where they were in relation to Kingston Road. They were on Blueberry Boulevard, so it would be six or seven blocks if he remembered his map accurately.

"Thanks, Bryan."

"You're welcome. Take the plague carrier with you." The other leader gathered his group with a word, and they started off in the opposite direction.

Roger wasn't sorry to see them go. His own small band gathered around him, looking to him for direction and he pointed to the east.

"We need a hole for the night. Dale, Ethan, you two search for a defensible spot and once you've found one, come back and get me and James. No use in all of us running around. Keep your radios on."

"If we run into a murder?" Dale asked.

"Run like your life depends on it because it does."

They nodded and took off.

"James." Roger looked down at the young man near his feet. "We need to talk."

"You're going to ask questions I can't answer, aren't you?"

"I need to know what you know. No matter how little you think it will help. I need to know because I'm risking my life to help you. Not just mine, but those of two kids I've come to think of as my own. Don't bullshit me, okay? I need to know how bad this is going to be."

"I can't tell you what I don't know, but I'll try to help. Where do you want me to start?" James pulled himself to a sitting position.

"Start with how you and Alice met and tell me the long story of your journey, if you don't mind. There might be something useful."

The pair moved off to the side of the street and into an abandoned store front. They could see the street, but it would be harder to see them as the light slowly diminished. Dale and Ethan didn't have much time to find somewhere they could really hide. While Roger might have used the store, the plate glass window was just too much for his fear. It might take a few hits, but it would not take nearly enough in order to make it a decent barricade.

James managed to lever himself up into a booth and lean against the table. He looked at Roger with sad eyes.

"I woke up looking into Alice's eyes."

CHAPTER TEN

Awakening to a New Day

JAMES COUGHED BEFORE OPENING HIS EYES, all too aware of having a nose full of dust and the stink of something he was certain he didn't want to identify. When he opened his eyes, there was a woman looking down at him. Her eyes, they were the pretty eyes he noticed. The second thing he noticed was they weren't identical. Not in the normal way most people have differing eyes. Instead, her eyes were two different colors. He blinked slowly as he took her in. Then she spoke.

"Hi."

"Hi," he replied. "What happened?" His voice sounded coarse, like unfinished wood, to his own ears. He could only imagine what it sounded like to her as she recoiled ever so slightly.

"They came," she said simply, and then she stepped over him and out of his immediate field of vision. James turned his head, trying to find her, then awkwardly flopping over on his side to see further. She had withdrawn to a window; the glass was smashed down in front of it as if someone had thrown a rock through it. "They came." The repetition did nothing for him. James stared at her numbly before reaching forward and starting to crawl despite the handful of glass he got first.

It took him a few moments to realize what the smell was in his nostrils: death. The recreation room of Southville Assisted Living, or Southie as James had heard it called, was empty aside from James, the woman at the window, and one of the orderlies. The young man looked fine, at least until James put his fingers in the blood previously spread across the floor. It was black and tacky like tar, clinging to his fingertips. It came from a wound in the side of the young man's head. The shotgun he had used was only an inch from his fingers.

"He decided not to fight." The woman watched James as he looked at the body with disbelief written across his features. "It was the easier way."

"What happened?" The question came out again. Her previous answer had done nothing for him. Instead, it only awakened panic in his breast. Who were the 'they' she referred to? Where had they come from?

"What's your name?" She ignored his question, and crossed the room, picking up the shotgun next to the body as she went. At the glass doors, she kicked a chair in front of them, then got down on one knee and poked the barrel of the shotgun through one of the holes in the door.

Looking down at the body in front of him, James replied," James." It was the name on the young man's badge.

"Good morning, James. Welcome to the rest of your life. However long that may be." The shotgun punctuated her sentence.

He wasn't sure he'd ever heard a shotgun discharge before. Now he wasn't sure if he would ever forget it. He covered his head and waited for it to be over, or to die, whichever came first.

The fight lasted a mere five minutes, but like every description he had ever heard about warfare, it seemed to take so much longer. Yet James stayed in one place, buried his face in the floor and pretended he was just listening to a movie playing in the next room as grunts and groans sounded out over the shotgun blasts and later the reports of a single pistol. Where had all the ammunition come from came the idle thought. A long moment of silence stretched out around him only to be snipped off by the sound of a gun once again going off. After that last shot, there were no more, and a shoe nudged him in the ribs.

"Ready to go?" At some point, he'd pissed himself. The acrid smell mingled with the blood; however, he was thankful for it. It was something that didn't smell of death. Dead people didn't pee.

"Where are we going?" he asked.

"East." Then she lifted him, putting him into a wheelchair. "We have to go East."

"What's East?"

"I don't know, but down in my bones, I know we have to go East."

"What's your name?" James asked.

"Alice." She pulled out the necklace and showed it to him. Alice in cursive made out of gold wire hung on a gold chain. "Let's go, James."

"Are we going to take anything else?"

"Why?"

"I don't know. Food? Water? Medicine? A change of clothes?"

"Do we need it?" Alice pushed him down the halls with a quickness he was not sure he'd have been able to match with a motor.

"I'd like a change of clothes, yes," he remarked as they came near his room. "Just stop for a second and at least help me change my pants?"

Alice relented, stopping in a room along the hall. James managed to find some pants and underwear that fit, they were his, but he didn't remember that, and with some assistance and a couple of fits of nervous laughter, they managed to get him dressed again.

"Thank you," he said.

"You're welcome. Now can we go?"

The body count was worse outside. Birds moved in flocks when they passed. James stared at what he saw, thrown back in his chair by the enormity of it. Alice simply pushed him along. She seemed blind to it. People from all manners of life were strewn across the ground like pickup sticks, some obviously caught in a vulnerable moment such as getting out of the car with groceries.

His stomach rumbled some at the smell of rotten oranges.

"Alice, what happened? You said they came, but I don't understand."

"James." She stopped the wheelchair and moved to where they could look eye to eye. "They, the zombies, came. They came, they ate or killed everyone. You and I are what's left of this town and now we have to go East. What we need is in the East."

"Did some angel tell you this?" James asked.

"No." For a moment, she stopped, seeming unsure for the first time since he'd met her only four or five hours earlier. "I just know. Come on." She took up the handles of his chair again and started pushing. He could only go along.

The chair made it a hundred miles before it had to be abandoned in favor of their lives. Alice was running, pushing him along, and the way became too narrow. She snatched him up and kept running, leaving the wheelchair behind. They didn't pick up another for a long while.

Sometimes Alice ran from the creatures, other times, when she could put him down, she stood her ground and fought. He had known there was something different about her the first time she did that without a weapon. No gun, no nothing, yet she waded into the fight with her bare hands and made short work of those creatures swarming around her.

James had cried. There was blood in her hair, and he was certain she was going to turn into one of those things. Yet she just picked him up and they kept moving.

"What's the matter?" They were some distance from the fight when she asked, undoubtedly noticing his occasional sniffles.

"You're going to turn into one of those things." He tried not to sob, and only partially succeeded. "A zombie."

"No, I'm not." She stopped walking, put him down on the hood of an abandoned car and showed him the bite marks on her arm. They were already closed. "I don't think I can."

James grabbed her arm and looked at it as if it had changed colors. It was markedly redder than it had been, but that was the splashing blood.

"How?"

"I don't know. I don't think you can either though because you'd been bitten when I found you. Had a nice livid mark on your neck, but you never got up snarling. That's why I didn't leave you. You didn't turn."

"Does it have something to do with our eyes?"

"I don't know about that either. I just happen to know that neither of us turned and so far, even through continued exposure, neither of us have. I think we might be immune. Maybe even something more?"

"I'd say a lot more since, you know, most people don't smash faces with one punch. No offense, but you don't look strong enough to do that."

"None taken." Alice picked him up again and started walking, this time holding him against her hip like one would a small child. "James, how did you lose your legs?"

The question he assumed would come up eventually, but he had no answer so when she asked, he shrugged.

"I don't know. I think it was an accident, but the memory won't pull up. I don't know why." There were a lot of places where he couldn't be certain what he had known or didn't know at any point in time. Now, they had been traveling together for over a week and they knew about as much about each other now as they had when they had first exchanged names. He been laid on the Southville Assisted Living Facility floor when he awoke to find her standing over him. "What about you? How did you get to Southville?"

"I just remember waking up there. I woke up lying on the floor in a pool of someone's vomit. I know it wasn't mine because the smell was a shock. Usually if you vomit, there is no shock when the smell hits you."

"Don't get hung-over much, do you?" James chuckled.

"Not that I can remember, but like you, there is an awfully big gap in what I remember." The walk down the street was slow, but they were still making good time. Either that or the sun wasn't moving. He wasn't entirely sure which of those was happening. "We're going to find the answers we need in the East."

"I'm glad you're sure about that."

"I'm glad to be sure about something." Both lapsed into silence at the same time. The steady thump of Alice's shoes against the pavement kept time with his thoughts.

"Alice, do you think things will ever get better?" It took him an hour to ask another question. Prompted by the sight of yet another body, a child. Once it had been a child anyway, now it was a soulless corpse abandoned by the side of the road with a hole through its torso where you could see the concrete.

"I don't know the answer to that one either. We'll find out when we make it East."

CHAPTER ELEVEN

The Search for Alice

"OUR CONVERSATIONS WERE PRETTY MUCH always like that." James stopped talking, looking at his drumming fingertips on the tabletop. He started to tap at some point in the story without realizing and now he looked at his moving fingers as though they didn't belong to him. "There is so much we don't know, but if we keep going East, we'll find answers. I believed her because I didn't have anything else to believe in. Now she's gone." He put his head down on the table with a moan. "Now she's gone."

"So, you keep going East," Roger offered.

The story wasn't too much different from the one James had told him earlier, waking up looking into Alice's eyes, fighting off the hordes, occasionally having a conversation about the end of the world or perhaps one could call it the beginning of the new one. "She would have wanted that, right?"

"Yes, she would have wanted us to keep going. But I can't go by myself."

The sun outside the store was now fully orange, golden in its final moments as the curls of violet appeared at the horizon. The street beyond the store front was empty, the soft cry of wind sounding like a lost soul as it moved over the pavement.

"You're not by yourself, James. You've got me, Ethan, and Dale. We'll be with you. It's not like we have anywhere else to go or something else to do."

"Thanks, that just makes me feel so very confident in your thoughts of my ideas." James hadn't bothered to pick his head up off the table.

"James, chill out, okay?" Running footsteps approached and Roger's radio crackled.

"Roger," said Dale.

He reached up to his shoulder and pressed the comm button. "Hey Dale, situation?"

"Situation's fine. Found a hiding spot. Access to water, decent food supply, and sturdy walls. Looks like the group using it moved on at some point. Where are you and James?"

"Inside a store near where we started. I'll meet you out front. Did you leave Ethan behind?"

"No, we're together. Thought it would go better with him to carry James and you and me to cover our asses."

"Good girl, thinking ahead." Roger's praise got a chuckle, then the comm went silent. "Come on." He directed the comment at James. "Let's meet them out front."

"Sure." If nothing else, James's recitation of his story had subdued his temper. That was plenty when you considered how much he rubbed people the wrong way. He crawled out of the booth and brushed his hair out of his face before starting to crawl along the littered floor.

"We've got to get you some arm protection if you're going to keep doing this."

"There's an idea." Even that didn't hold its expected venom. "I miss Alice."

"I can only guess how much."

"Yeah, I suppose you don't understand at all." He moved across the floor at a pace a little faster than a snail, but Roger was not in any hurry. Ethan and Dale were outside by the time they got to the door.

"We ready?" Roger asked because he couldn't think of what else to say.

The perils of being in leadership, occasionally you had to ask the thoroughly obvious. Ethan worked on getting James up and in a comfortable position. Dale gave him one of those long suffering looks that said she was trying to restrain herself from saying something which would be damaging to his ego. "All right then," he said after a moment of, uncomfortable for him, silence. "Let's move out. Dale, you've got point. Ethan middle. I'm taking up the rear."

They caravanned out of the parking lot. It took just about ten minutes to get to the new spot and it was in the correct direction, so Roger mentally thanked goodness it would be easier once they got started the next morning. Once, it had been a house. Now it was more like a fortress with the reinforced walls along the front of the house. The backyard housed a converted garden cemetery. Apparently, they wanted to bury their own close by. Roger had to wonder if they cut off their heads before they put them in the coffins to avoid them coming back again. He immediately pushed the thought away.

Once upon a time, the living room had been an entertaining space. He could tell that from the arrangement of the chairs and the carpet. It brought back a thought of evenings when he would watch decorating shows with his wife for ideas of things they could do to their own space. Back when he had a wife, a son, a house, a dog, and a life that didn't include killing former people in order to keep from becoming a former person himself. James had plopped himself down on the couch and looked as if he were going to go to sleep. No one would blame him. He'd been going for quite a while and moving from denial to acceptance in the death of his closest friend was probably more emotionally exhausting than Roger cared to admit.

Ethan crashed about in the kitchen. Dale had gone upstairs to investigate what was going on there. Hopefully nothing. Roger moved into the kitchen and set his weapon down on the counter.

"There's no fruit," Ethan said and stuck his head back out of the pantry. "And nothing to make bread with, but there are some canned vegetables and a freezer full of meat. Not sure how much of it has succumbed to freezer burn though."

"Find out. Then we can make some decisions about dinner and how much we're taking with us."

"We're going to get Alice, but that's not far, we can just come back here," Ethan said.

"No, we're going East after we bury Alice properly. Supposedly there are some answers as to what is going on."

"You know the only thing truly East is the ocean, right?" Ethan looked up at him.

"Well, then we'd better hope that whatever we're going to find shows up before we get to the beach."

The sound of the water heater rumbling to life spooked them both into reaching for weapons. A nervous chuckle ran between them.

"Dale." The name came out in unison.

"Typical woman," Ethan added.

"Oh, shut up." Roger waved his gun at him, openly showing his finger was not on the trigger. "You need one, so expect to be taking one when she gets finished. Let's see if we can scavenge some more clothes. Things that don't smell like the sewer."

When Roger went back into the living room, James was sound asleep and even starting to snore in his position on the couch. Roger envied him for a moment, certain he wanted a good long nap. No, what he really wanted was to wake up and realize that this whole thing had been some horrid nightmare and his wife was lying there beside him dreaming of the duvet color she was going to buy at the Black Friday sale. He wanted to wake up and walk into his son's room, pick the boy up, and hug him until he protested "I can't breathe, Daddy" to make him stop. Roger sank down into the chair opposite the couch and watched the slow rise and fall of James's chest while he slept.

Once upon a time, before the zombies...

The phrase occurred to him, rather like a fairy tale opener, and he let himself smile a sick, exhausted smile. Then he closed his eyes. The rest of the night disappeared into darkness.

Morning peeked in through the windows, carrying with it a hope for something better. Unfortunately, that same hope had been reappearing for the better part of a year without any realization things were going to change. One, long nightmare shared among heaven only knew how many people. The United States was cut off by an ocean. How had Europe fared? Was there still a Europe? These were the questions that woke Roger up. The questions and the smell of something frying.

He opened his eyes and looked at the couch. James was gone. The sounds of footfalls told him someone was nearby, but he couldn't be sure who it was. Well, James was automatically ruled out, but whether it was Ethan or Dale he didn't know. Getting up, he stretched, popping his neck as he did.

"Getting old," he muttered. "Getting too old for this sort of thing."

"Hardly." Dale appeared at his elbow with a plate in one hand. "Here." She shoved it at him. On the plate was some strange colored sausage and what looked like a piece of fried potato.

"They were growing potatoes out back and the sausage seemed okay, so Ethan cooked it."

"Ethan cooked?" Roger eyed the plate and the accompanying food as though it had just been delivered to him by an unknown alien of questionable origin.

"Yeah. Don't worry. We made James try it first to make sure it was safe. He's scarfing the stuff down like tomorrow isn't coming."

"Are we sure it is?"

"Did you wake up on the wrong side of the bed this morning?" Dale rolled her eyes at him in a way that made him think of pre-teen daughters getting upset at their parents. "What's with the doom and gloom? Yesterday, you were all let's go do this."

"Actually, that was Ethan. I was trying to be the voice of reason."

"The voice of reason would have had us still in a prison cell waiting to be a zombie buffet." Ethan came around the corner with James peeking over his shoulder.

"Ate all the food." James looked content. It was a new face on him from Roger's perspective. "Do you want that?"

"Yes, I want my breakfast." Roger moved his plate protectively out of reach. "Thanks."

He flopped back into the chair and started eating. The others disappeared to their own corners. He didn't pay much attention to it. Nothing was crashing or breaking. No one was screaming. He absorbed the peaceful moment. It almost felt normal. All he needed was something on the blank television at one end of the living room.

The television was snowy. There was no signal. The plate was empty before he truly had time to think about it. He stared at it for a moment and the faint traces of grease seemed to beckon him to lick the plate.

He put it down on the coffee table and looked out the window through the curtains. The street beyond was empty. It was actually a good spot. They could stay here and maybe make something that approximated at life. Except if they did, there was no telling what would happen to Alice's body and they would never find the promised answers held in the East. Did he really believe there were answers somewhere out there?

"Yeah," he answered his internal thought process aloud and levered himself up out of the chair again with a grunt. "Y'all ready to move out?"

The question was asked loud enough to be heard to the edges of their little abode. Within thirty seconds, he had three pairs of eyes looking at his. Looking at them, he took in their faces as if to memorize them for their memorial.

ALICE

"Let's move out." They left the little house behind. Alice was waiting. She might well wait forever, but why should they make her wait that long?

By noon, they reached the gate near Kingston Road. The sun, high above, beat down on them and made their equipment seem even heavier. Roger stuck his head down into the manhole, expecting something to come snarling up out of the dark at him. His expectations were not met. There was a sigh of relief for that.

"Okay, we're here." He stopped them and showed them the darkness below. "We've got to go down, same formation as before. Keep it tight. Keep the safety's off. Don't point at each other, all the usual jazz."

"Yes, Dad." Roger shot James a nasty look which was met with a sarcastic smile.

"Have I said I hate you lately?"

"Not to me. I think you told Ethan that back when he decided to drop me on the hood of a pretty Chevy so that he could take a piss."

"Hey, I'm the one carrying you. Don't get me into trouble or you can get where you're going on your own." Ethan's threat was empty, but he said it anyway.

"I know and then you're slowed down to my pace which is about the speed a snail is going to be able to travel in a year. Do you want to wait that long in order to be able to reach our goal?"

Ethan shut up, leaving each of them to their own thoughts until Roger motioned for Dale to head down the hole in front of them. She was the point person. Roger was bringing up the rear, as usual. Ethan and James between them. James held onto Ethan's back and tried not to be too much of a burden when it came right down to it, for all his attitude.

"Nothing down here!" Dale shouted up from the bottom.

Ethan helped James down into the hole and then followed him, leaving Roger at the top alone for a few seconds. Roger looked up into the sky and marked the position of the sun again. It was noon. They would be out of the hole long before dark. They would have Alice's body by then. Things would go exactly as planned and then they could take off for the East. East was the answer. East would take away the murders and they would all be free once again to stop living like rabbits in fear of the fox.

Roger scooted down the hole and was surprised to find Dale and James at the bottom with Ethan nowhere in sight.

"Where'd he go?" Roger asked.

"Took off running down the tunnel. Didn't say anything, just took off running."

James leaned against the wall and shrugged when Roger looked at him.

"We're going to have to find him. Neither of us can carry James all that far." Dale rolled her eyes at his concern as if she had already thought about that and was offended at his inference that she hadn't.

"Leave me here," James offered from his position. "I can manage for a little while on my own. Besides, Rog, it's possible I can't catch this shit anyway, so I'm actually safer than any of you."

ALICE

"Good point." Roger tossed him a pistol. "Something comes, squeeze off a few shots and let us know, okay?"

"Yeah, yeah. Go find Ethan."

Roger and Dale took off down the tunnel following Ethan's previous path. The tunnel was dank and smelled of death. Occasionally there were bodies, but they seemed as if they had been washed there rather than died there. Whether or not that was a good thing, neither of them knew, but Ethan was somewhere ahead of them.

The dumping ground was felt before it was seen as if the weight of the collected spiritual leavings had taken on a physical presence and saturated the air. Roger brought his weapon up at movement ahead of him. Dale was at his elbow and she did the same. He could barely make out Ethan's voice.

"You're not dead." Ethan's voice greeted them. It was soft, quiet, caressing, as if speaking to someone sleeping. "You're not dead. You didn't leave us."

"Has he gone fruit loops?" Dale whispered to Roger.

Roger shrugged and shook his head. Whatever happened, he was not sure. However, what they saw next was enough to challenge his thinking about everything else.

Ethan had found Alice. He knelt atop the bodies piled around her, holding her, and stroking her hair away from her forehead as if she were fast asleep.

"You didn't leave us," Ethan said.

Alice's fingertips twitched, and then her fingers curled into a fist.

"You didn't die." Ethan whispered.

Her head moved, snapping to one side as if she had been slapped.

"You didn't leave us."

Alice sat up, her head hanging forward. She looked like she'd been propped up in that position. Then she lifted her chin. Her eyes were open but glazed. She put one hand down, putting her weight on it and pushed herself to stand up.

"James?" The name was a question.

"He's waiting on you, Alice." Ethan moved closer and put his arm around her. "He's waiting. I had to leave him behind. We had to hurry."

Dale and Roger watched with wide eyes. She got up. She was walking and talking.

"They shot you." Dale didn't bother trying to keep her voice down now. Who was going to hear them? The dead people? "How?"

Alice's voice was gritty, broken, but she was talking. The blur in her eyes was clearing as she looked at them. "Can't leave James by himself for long."

"Alice." Roger held up one hand to bring her to a stop. "We need to talk."

"Get James. Go East."

"Alice, we need to talk."

The woman crawled off the bodies in the direction of the exit where they had left James. "Need to get to James."

"Alice!" Roger shouted.

She stopped.

"We need to talk to you." Roger brought his voice back down to a moderate level.

She took off running, leaving the three of them behind, leaving them no choice but to start running in hopes of catching her. By the time they made it back to the manhole, Alice was already there with James.

"Alice." Roger called her name with his best teacher authority voice and was surprised when she looked up. "What is going on?"

She picked up James as if he were nothing.

"I missed you," he said.

"I didn't miss you, but I was dead, so I suppose it doesn't count." She pressed her nose against his neck and closed her eyes. "I'm glad you're okay though, if that means anything."

"It means a lot." He closed his eyes as well and for a moment. They looked almost like a pair of lovebirds. So long as no one paid attention to the blood in Alice's hair. "Don't get shot again, please?"

"I will make every attempt."

Then she started up the ladder, James holding on around her neck. The group trailed back to the little house they'd occupied the night before and shut themselves in.

One more night in relative peace wouldn't be so bad.

CHAPTER TWELVE

We Need a Map

ROGER AWOKE THE NEXT MORNING TO FIND the others asleep, save one. Alice sat up, looking through the front window's curtains. He left her in that exact position the night before.

"Did you sleep?"

"I slept. I was dead," Alice said.

Her terse reply told him that subject while not off limits was still sore and touchy. Best to leave it be at least until the end of the day. Assuming Alice developed better moods. She moved in and out of moods rather rapidly.

"I talked to James," Roger said.

Alice narrowed her mismatched eyes.

"He said we should go East, and I remember you saying much the same thing." Roger settled on the couch near her, but out of immediate arm's reach. Not that he truly expected that to help much when considering a woman who moved like a striking cobra. She smelled like the bottom of a snake pit. He reminded himself to tell her she could go shower since there was still some water pressure left. If nothing else, they could at least bail out the back of the toilet and let her rinse some of the stink off that way. "You even said it once or twice while you were crawling off the heap underground. So, I have to ask. What's in the East?"

"You asked before. I don't know."

He wasn't sure if what he heard was regret or not. Her face didn't change either way, so it was hard to be certain.

"What do you know?" Roger asked.

"Nothing." She almost whispered the word across the space between them before leaning in. "I know *nothing*. I *feel* something. Something screaming in my blood. It screams East."

She sounded weary. Alice levered herself up out of the chair and walked over to where James lay on the floor half-covered by a blanket which proudly proclaimed its former owner to be an adherent to the University of Alabama Roll Tide congregation. He appeared to be peaceful, even childlike in his sleep. She knelt next to him and smoothed his black hair away from his face. "East is all I know. Answers or ends, I don't know which, but East I know."

"Then we need a map," Roger said. He pursed his lips in thought. "And to get moving. Being above ground makes us easy targets."

She nodded, reached down, and pinched James's nose closed. He snorted, snuffled, threw back his head, and then opened his eyes. Blinking, he looked up at Alice with confusion.

"Trying to teach me about being dead?" James croaked.

With a shake of her head, she got up and moved over to Ethan who opened his eyes to look at her.

"Hi, you stink." Ethan said, waving a hand across his nose.

"So, I do," she admitted.

"I packed most of the food, so I guess I'll unpack it and make breakfast, then we can get out of here." Ethan uncovered himself and moved to stretch as Alice went to Dale who was shaking herself awake as well.

"Cold breakfast. Get up, get your gear, we'll eat on the run. We've already been here too long." Roger's anxiousness communicated itself to the others. They put back on what little combat gear they had. It was good stuff, as long as you didn't get into a straight up hand to hand with anything overly nasty.

"But I'm hungry now," James complained as Alice lifted him and shifted him into their standard carry position. Alice just rolled her eyes and humped the two of them toward the door.

"Woah, hold on." Roger put his arm out to stop her. "Gun on point. You can bring up second, if you want."

Roger motioned for Dale to precede them out of the house with Ethan right behind her. Daylight greeted them out on the street with the same enthusiasm it had shown inside the house, bright and warm. Without the guns and the stink of blood, it might have been a holiday, a group getting together to go have some fun. With the guns, it seemed like a forced march. With the blood, it was a retreat from a rout. They fell into a loose line, Dale on point, less than a hundred yards ahead but ahead just the same. Alice carried James halfway back to Roger, who walked along but kept throwing glances back. Ethan ranged along beside them, his eyes darting back and forth across the street waiting for something to happen.

They all waited for something to happen.

They were part way up Seventh Street when Roger spotted a gas station and whistled Dale to a stop. She turned to look at him with a confused expression he could read even across the distance. He indicated the gas station with his gun and then moved toward it, giving Dale and Ethan the fist-sign of stay put.

ALICE

Alice followed him toward the darkened building. A bright red sports car sat out front. The door hung wide by one hinge. A white paneled van remained in the handicapped space. The brown handprints streaking down the sides made it less than pristine along with the touches of rust from long years of use. Roger concentrated on the rust and moved toward the gas station's glass paneled doors. A little window that led to a counter bore smears of things Roger didn't want to think about, but they were intact.

"Funny these are still good," Roger commented.

Alice grunted in response and James swiveled his head to look at Roger as he opened the door.

"Stop."

"What?" Roger asked.

"Something moved beyond the glass. Back up." By the time, James spoke again, Alice was going for the door. A shape hit the glass doors with a thump, adding a fresh smear to the multitude. It was human-ish. They took too long. Ethan and Dale waited at the edge of the parking lot.

"Should I shoot it?" Roger asked.

"And risk drawing attention to ourselves?" James said. "Alice?"

She waited until the thing moved away from the door and then jerked the glass obstruction out of its way. It fell forward onto the pavement leading into the gas station. Alice put her foot down on the creature, killing its attempt to wriggle away. She followed that with a soccer-ball-kick to its face which broke its neck. At some point, someone had taken out its legs and left it without quite enough leverage to strike the windows.

"James, down." Alice ordered.

"Why?"

She took her hands out from under him and let him hang there a moment before slipping out of his grip.

"Stay here with them." She made a stay-down motion and stalked past the glass door.

Inside the gas station, the tiled floor was a mess of blood, chips, soda, and liquor. It crunched and squelched under her shoes. The expected electrical hum typically underscoring all gas stations was absent. But something made noise.

Outside, James sat on the pavement, scanning the exterior of the building until he noticed something near the white paneled van. Roger watched as James went toward it.

"Where are you going?" Roger asked.

"To see something," James said.

His upper half disappeared into the area right behind the van's front tires. Roger could hear him crawling, scuffing against the pavement. Roger waved Ethan and Dale over to him. He headed around the van, weapon at the ready. On the far side, James came out from under the van. Roger looked at what he was crawling toward. Someone had parked a motorcycle so close to the van they hadn't seen it from the road.

James, his lower half still under the van, caressed one of the wheels and murmured, "I remember this."

Those words had barely floated from his throat when his head dropped forward with the snap of his teeth coming together, hard.

"James." Roger trotted the distance, slinging his weapon back on its strap with little thought. He dropped down next to James and felt his neck for a pulse. It was there. Roger breathed out slowly trying to pull his racing heart from its quick pace. He turned as Ethan and Dale appeared at his elbow. "We've got to get him out from under there."

"We'll have to pull him back the way he came, that bike's too heavy to move," said Dale.

"Get on it. We're exposed out here," Roger said.

By the time they managed to get James pulled back underneath the van, Alice stood in the convenience store's doorway. She watched them work and scanned the road at times like a dog scenting the air. As Ethan struggled to get James's dead weight off the ground, she came over to pick up her friend.

"Man, he's even heavier than he was. I didn't think that was possible." Ethan grunted.

The group relocated to inside the store. The day's shadows crept toward sunset.

Bodies littered the floor.

Not exactly a surprise. Ethan stepped over a woman with most of her face missing. From the torn nylons and blood tipped hands, he figured she had gone zombie before someone had, not so politely, put her out of her misery. Dale was a touch surprised to find several newspapers strewn over something toward the back of the store. As she reached out to touch them, Roger stopped her, and gestured to something she had only barely seen but hadn't registered. It was a bright pink Ked the size of half a slice of bread. A kid's shoe.

He shook his head and stepped away. Alice propped James in a sitting position on the counter and appeared to be studying his face. He looked peaceful as though he were sleeping, though his face flashed expressions. A grimace. A smile. What might have been silent laughter. Yet his eyes didn't open.

"Ethan! Dale!" The two looked at Roger as he called their names. "Check to see what we can carry with us. I'm going to find a map."

He looked at Alice, holding her friend, nodded, and then moved around her looking for the map carousel he expected to be there. Ethan shoved the entire contents of the beef jerky section into his pack. Dale made a face.

"How do you know any of that stuff is still good?" she asked him.

"With the preservatives in it, it's shelf stable for years." Ethan returned as he started checking the expiration dates on the cans in another aisle.

"How do you know that?" she asked.

"Stock boy small talk. I used to work in a grocery store. Gotta have something to talk about when sports and girls no longer appeals." He chucked a can of soup over his shoulder. "They've got to rotate their stock better. That stuff expired two years ago." It landed with a *thud* and rolled to the base of the cooler. Dale followed it with her eyes before going to the cooler door.

"Bottled water, you think?" she asked.

"Yeah. We're going to need something once we get out of the city," Ethan replied turning a can over in his hands.

Dale opened the case and reached in.

A hand, appearing out of the dark like a movie tentacle, grabbed her by the wrist. Behind it, a pair of flat angry eyes glittered in the cooler's darkness. There were other eyes with it.

Dale screamed.

Another set of hands shot forward in a different space, bumping against the glass of the cooler. Then another. The hand holding Dale developed a broken twin, a chewed through stump still trying to grab.

Though it had her dominant hand, Dale managed to bring her gun up and fire, but she couldn't get it high enough for a head shot. Ethan, who had dropped what he was doing all over the floor, got to her in time to hear the first shot up close. They were all going to be deaf before this was over. He got the headshot Dale missed, and then he had to drop his weapon to grab Dale. She'd been dragged hard against the shelves by a body refusing to let her go as it collapsed. Other hands were reaching, scrabbling for purchase.

Dale watched, her eyes wide, waiting for the injury which would end her life. Her skin was still unbroken.

"Roger!" Ethan screamed.

It wasn't Roger who was suddenly there but Alice. She grabbed Ethan by the waist and pulled him backward, dragging Dale and part of the zombie along with them. Some of the shelving fell askew, crashing in place to make a gaping hole. The zombie which had lost its grip on Dale, attempted to wedge its shoulders further in, teeth snapping on the empty air. It received a solid kick to the face for its trouble. Then Alice slammed the door shut. The front of its skull collapsed toward the back of its head with a sound like a popped balloon.

"Thank you." Dale gasped as Alice snatched her up off the ground. The strange woman didn't acknowledge the thanks but rather turned over both of Dale's hands and ran dirty fingers up Dale's arms.

Not even a scratch.

Behind her, zombies tried to crawl through the hole in the cooler and found a stout glass door in front of them.

"We'll have to get water somewhere else," Dale said. Her voice quivered.

"Maybe they have a stockroom in the back. We can check," Ethan said wrapping his arms around her shoulders. It wasn't quite a hug, but close.

Roger watched Alice approach from where he stood with James's body propped up against his back. Roger had a map, folded until it was nothing more than their city and the Eastern coast. If he understood what he was looking at, they had a long way to go in order to go East as Alice insisted. He thrust the map at the woman.

"Do any of these names look familiar?"

Alice leaned, then shuffled around until she could look over his shoulder and read the words right side up.

Templeton. Andersville. Cartertown. Sarasota. St. Petersburg. Cairo. Kennedy. Watson.

Roger listened to her breathe, slow, rhythmic, and regular stop abruptly before she stabbed a finger against the page.

"There."

Senora.

According to the map's legend, it was a small town, barely large enough to register as anything other than a name. Right on the ocean. In fact, from what he saw, the most eastern point on the map.

Putting his finger on the town, he drew a line toward the west, looking for a road. The nearest major highway didn't come close, but a smaller, older highway snaked its way along the coast near the town. A smaller coastal highway that ran through the eastern edge of the city they stood in. Without calculating, Roger estimated they could walk the distance.

James awoke with a shiver. It ran from the crown of his head to his hips and stopped. He blinked, then dug his chin into Roger's shoulder.

"Thanks for being my pillow," James said.

"You're awake. Now get off me," Roger said.

James sat back against the Plexiglas barrier separating the cash register from the rest of the store and Roger stepped away.

"Are you okay?" Alice asked, her eyes said she was concerned.

Roger glanced back.

James looked confused. Then he said," I thought I remembered something." He paused, closing his eyes and shook his head. "Something bad."

James held his arms out to Alice in the child's gesture of pick me up. She obliged. "It had to do with that motorcycle and my legs."

"There's only one thing motorcycles do that end you up like this," Ethan said. He and Dale had made it back from the storeroom behind the cooler. It had been an eerie moment, trying not to think about how thick the walls were keeping the zombies inside the cooler and away from the two of them, but they had made it.

"What's that?" James asked.

Roger watched James's face, uncertain if the boy was making a joke or not. Ethan answered the question with a shrug.

"Crash," Ethan said.

James shivered again, mismatched eyes rolling backward in his head. Then he was with them again.

"I crashed." The words came out slow as if James worked them around in his brain and his mouth in an uncharacteristic way. He blinked, multiple times, then brought his hands to his face. "I crashed." There were those words again, said in the wondrous voice of someone who is half-dreaming or trying to enunciate the impossible. Except this was a simple reality. "The crash broke my back and I..."

He stopped again, and he looked up into Alice's face hard. "You."

"Me?"

"I." The word stuck on his tongue and then he swallowed it down again.

"I lost it."

"What happened to you, James?" Dale asked.

"I don't remember anymore. I can sorta see the crash. All foggy in my head until that super bright spot of pain right there at the end and then there's something past it, but it's too hazy. It's gone." He curled tighter in Alice's arms, hiding his face against her chest. Alice rocked him, back and forth, like a baby.

Roger watched them both for a moment. "We need to get out of here. We're too exposed."

The others nodded, the group in agreement.

"Let's make some time and find a better hiding spot before it gets too dark. All this glass is making me nervous," Roger said.

"Still makes you wonder how it stayed intact," Dale said.

"No food," Alice said.

None of them had to ask Alice what she meant by that.

The sunshine progressed toward late afternoon. The prelude to twilight, the time when all those who preferred not to become zombie chow bedded down in fortified positions if they had one. Roger waved Dale back into the point position and directed Ethan to take up the rear. He would walk with Alice and James.

"You said the name, Senora, was familiar." Roger returned to their previous conversation.

Alice made no response.

"Why is it familiar?"

Still nothing.

"Alice, I need you to talk to me."

"She doesn't know," James said looking up at Alice's chin. She carried him in silence. "And I don't either."

Roger stopped in the middle of the street. Alice moved a few strides ahead before turning around.

"We risked our necks for you," Roger said.

She tilted her head to one side, then the other.

"We've risked everything to help you."

Dale and Ethan closed ground toward the small knot.

"And you're not telling us everything," Roger added.

Alice adjusted James until she could look into his eyes and after a moment's communion turned and started walking again. James settled down in her arms. If he'd put his thumb in his mouth, he would truly look like a baby.

"Alice," Roger called after her.

"No," she replied. "I didn't ask you for anything. I told you everything. I know where I have to go. I am going. Come or stay."

The day wore on. Alice walked away. Roger looked from her back to Dale and Ethan who had joined him on the pavement. They watched Alice and James leave. Ethan looked as though he would start after them any second.

"This is your call," Roger said.

"We know," Ethan said. "We know, but." He stopped. "Can they make it on their own?"

"Better question, without Central, can we make it without them?" Dale asked.

Alice's shadow grew long, and, in the light, her body seemed to merge with it becoming a single black column. James's body served as a crossbar.

Roger swallowed past a lump in his throat and tried to ignore the itching in the back of his head. It had always been there, that itch, though it had been quiet for some time. The itch to know and to understand. There it was again, sudden as a poison ivy rash on his brain, and the only things that could soothe it were knowing why and what. Why had this happened and what was going to happen next? Alice might not have known why, but she knew where to find an answer and was willing to bet her life on it. With a sigh, Roger started walking. The other two fell into step behind him.

"Ethan, run ahead and catch her. We're going to have to find somewhere to hold up soon." He watched the boy go running forward, and then turned to look at the girl by his side. His kids.

He hoped to hell he wasn't working on getting them killed.

CHAPTER THIRTEEN

Getting on the Road

FOR THE EVENING, AN OLD BANK SERVED as their home. Built when banks took their architectural cues from castles instead of high-rises, it was all gray brick and mortar with small nearly inaccessible windows and only two obvious doors, one on the front and another on the back. Dale, once again on point, spotted the bank glowering from two doors in off the intersection in town. After placing James on the carpeted lobby floor, Alice and Ethan had taken a quick once over of the place while Dale and Roger found what passed for a break room. It had a sink, a double burner coffee pot, a fridge, and a small electric grill.

Everything sat disused. Like everything else, they appeared abandoned in the middle of things. Just like the people who saw them.

The fridge was a sight and a smell. Dale shut it quickly, unwilling to explore any further than the initial wall of sensory overload to find out if there was anything worth having in it. Roger had shaken his head and started looking in the pantry. They didn't really need food. The stuff from the convenience store would keep them at least a few days. What they really needed was a way to make food.

Not something they were going to find here.

By the time they got back, James scooted his way over to beneath the teller counter. He had taken a nail file and was busying himself with breaking into the drawers.

"It's not like we can use the money," remarked Dale.

"Not interested in money," he said, the tip of his tongue stuck out one side of his mouth like a cartoon lock picker. "Seeing if anyone carried a gun however might be more useful."

Roger just shook his head and watched Alice walk across the room, pick up what he could only assume was once the manager's desk, and heft it up on her shoulder. She walked the piece of wood back to the door they came in and set it down, lengthwise, against the portal, effectively shutting it from the inside.

"Good thinking," he murmured.

Ethan found himself a reception couch and started unpacking.

"Who wants the chips?"

"Me!" cried James. As if to punctuate his enthusiasm for faux-cheese snacks, the drawer he had been working on popped open with a snap and made a similarly loud connection with his head. "OW!" He rubbed away the dribble of blood.

"Well done," said Dale as she dropped down on the couch next to Ethan and took the bag of Cheetos James had asked for. "Find anything?"

"Nah, looks like they cleared out ahead of time."

Alice and Roger sat on the floor a few feet from each other when James scooted over, making dragging noises over the tile then fuzzier ones on the carpet. The heels on his shoes were more scuffed than the toes. Ethan tossed him a bag of corn chips and he settled to eating them with gusto.

"Alice?" Ethan offered her a bag and she waved it away. "Roger?" Roger opened his hands and caught the bag of Jerky Ethan tossed to him. "So, what's the plan?"

"The plan is to hit I-11." Roger stopped a moment to remember the information from the map. "And follow it north until we get to Cantor, then we'll strike out east for Senora."

"How far do you think it is?" Dale's question made him pull the map out of his pack.

"Hey, James, lend me a shoelace, will you?"

The rapid eating came to a halt as James looked him like a confused chipmunk all puffed out cheeks and big round eyes. Then he choked everything down, *thudded* his chest a time or two, and leaned over to grab a shoelace out of his scuffed shoes. The black lace looked as though it had been chewed at both ends, but it was long enough for Roger's purpose. Spreading the map on the floor, he measured out the distance.

"We've got about 700 miles to cover. Averaging maybe 20 miles a day, it'll take just over a month, if we're lucky."

Hope drained from the room with an inaudible sound.

Outside, the orange sun disappeared below the horizon and night dropped upon the world like a predator with no electric lights to keep it at bay. Inside, the darkness held less sway but not much.

"Might as well bed down. Morning's going to come early if it comes at all."

CHAPTER FOURTEEN

James's Nightmare

THE THRUMMING SOUND OF RAIN ON A HARD surface woke James or rather startled him into realizing he was already awake. He was hunched forward, hands on the handlebars of a motorcycle. His visor was up, the tint too dark in the sudden thunderstorm, and his face wet. He blinked away the encroaching rain and forced himself to keep the bike steady. He kept the bike upright even as the wheels slid ever so slightly out of alignment. The roadside was dotted with trees. He saw the silver flash of guardrails slip by. Under his breath, he sang. What was the name of that song again?

He didn't know.

The yellow sign signaled a sharp turn glared at him for his speed and James gave its back a grin. He could make this. Even in these conditions. The road slick, the bike wobbly, him punch drunk on too little sleep.

Except...

The part of his brain with the knowledge of his true current state, crippled and dependent, knew he didn't make it. The nightmare slowed as the second sign for the sharp curve floated into view, a yellow diamond warning him of

133

how his life would be forever altered by his coming actions. With a laugh, he pushed the bike to go faster. In the dream, it continued to coast along on rails, no faster or slower, as his fate came forward an inch at a time.

"Take my body to the river," he sang along as he banked into the turn. The bike slid, toppling sideways, taking him with it. A flash of pain ran through his leg as it shattered, then his side as the combined weight dragged him on the pavement shredding his jacket and some of the skin beneath. Around in a turn, he and his bike moved as dancers, off the side of the road until...

James sat up, a deep throb in his lower back making him grimace in pain. Alice was within arm's reach, lying on her back, face pointed to the ceiling, hands on her chest like a corpse in a coffin. James looked away, scanning the darkness for the others. Roger and Ethan had both claimed couches while Dale curled in the fetal position beneath the edge of the teller counter. She opened her eyes to look at him. Taking that as invitation, James scooted over to her and laid back down. Dale draped an arm over him and closed her eyes.

"I had a bad dream," he said.

"The whole world's a bad dream. Go back to sleep."

"No, a real bad dream, like a memory."

Dale rolled to face him and braced her hand next to his head to hold herself up.

"Seriously?" she asked.

"Yeah. I had an accident. It crippled me."

"I thought you said you didn't remember?"

"I didn't. I dreamed it just now. I was singing a song and I crashed my bike in the rain and my back broke against a tree and..." He took a breath. "And, I'm scared."

When Dale lowered herself down onto his chest, he wrapped his arms around her, hugging her close. She was almost small enough to be a teddy bear. Funny how tough she was. Then again, teddy bears had to be tough to take all the dragging around they got. So maybe it wasn't funny at all.

"I'm scared," James repeated.

"It's okay," she whispered, closing her eyes again. "We all are."

James shut his mouth over the retort and listened to Dale's heartbeat instead.

Throw my body in the river.

Dale slept on his chest. When James woke up again, the first trickles of dawn snuck in the windows. Alice sat up, looking at the desk blocking the door. Nearby, Roger studied the map as though the information had changed from the day before. Ethan remained asleep on his couch with his right-hand dangling protectively over his pack. When he shuffled himself into motion, Alice turned to look at him and even smiled. He smiled back, feeling a little bit of color rise, though he wasn't sure why. He rolled Dale onto her side and scooted across the floor to his companion, who threw one arm across him and drew him against her side.

"I had a dream last night," he said.

"I know. I heard you when you moved."

"You did?"

"Yes."

"Are you upset?"

"At what?"

"That." He didn't make any indications, but she knew what he meant. Alice shook her head and pressed a kiss to his forehead.

"Be careful of caring for her is all I will say. We may not be able to keep them," Alice said.

James didn't answer, turning to look at Roger who wasn't paying attention to anything around him.

"What's he got going on?"

"Something about the area we need to get through in order to make it out of town," Alice said with a shrug. "He foresees trouble."

All the King's horses and all the King's men will never rescue me. The words came to mind unbidden, but James knew them just the same.

"The river," he mumbled.

"What river?"

"I don't know. Just a song. A song I used to know."

"Used to know."

"Yeah, it was in the dream. I was singing it when I broke my back."

"Oh." Alice didn't ask another question. Instead she got up and knelt down near Roger.

"What's the trouble?" she asked.

"The area we're going to have to travel through was heavily populated when this whole mess started," Roger said.

"Which may mean heavily infested now," Alice continued.

"Exactly."

Alice appeared to ponder that for a moment, then shook her head.

"James needs transportation of his own. I'm not as effective when I have to carry him, and Ethan can't carry him for long enough to be feasible."

As if reacting to the sound of his name, Ethan sat up and stretched with a yawn. Dale had already started to wake up. James watched her gather her gear.

"We should have taken that van back at the convenience store," Roger said. "But we can't guarantee how far we'll get and there's no way of keeping it from becoming a rolling death trap if we get swarmed." He began to fold the map, a frown full on his face. "We'll have to come up with something as we go."

Alice nodded her agreement and stood up, stretching toward the ceiling. Her back popped with a sound like opening a soda can.

"Getting old, Alice?" James asked.

She glared at him with a raised eyebrow before scooping him up off the floor and spinning him, so his legs swung out behind him.

"Okay, I take it back!" James laughed, clinging to her chest.

"Thank you," she said putting him down.

Ethan tossed out energy bars. Roger caught his. Dale let hers hit the floor, not paying attention. Alice caught hers and James's one handed, then dropped James's into his lap. It was gone as soon as he could open it. Alice ate more slowly. Everyone got a bottle of water. Then Alice moved the desk to uncover the door and they headed out into the day.

Clouds built on the horizon, thick, charcoal gray, and nasty. A thunderstorm swept toward the city.

Roger shook his head at it and said, "We've got to make some time before that hits, so let's move out." He waved Ethan to the front. "Just keep following the street until I call a stop. We're going in the right general direction."

"Got it."

"Eyes open, both of you." He addressed Dale and Ethan. "Don't let yourself get cut off."

"We got it." Ethan nodded.

"Good. Get to it." The pair went in their separate directions, one covering point the other taking up the rear.

Roger and Alice exchanged a glance, then Alice asked, "What do you want me to do?"

He blinked.

"I don't know," he answered. "But I'm sure you'll come up with something when the time comes."

She nodded and started walking. A few steps later, Roger followed.

Every few minutes, James checked the position of the clouds rolling toward them like an advancing army. They were making good time. He had just gone back to looking over Alice's shoulder when Ethan put up the fist for a stop. Everyone froze. Ethan made the sign to take cover. The group ducked into various spaces created by traffic jammed cars and rubble. Though he was further from the front than Ethan, James could see the shadow of something coming out of a side street toward them. It lumbered into view, a humanoid shape of knitted bodies.

The creature from the cistern came to mind immediately but this wasn't quite the same. James saw Ethan duck down further merging into the shadow of the car he hid behind. The creature's head swung, attached by little more than a thread of skin and bone, eyes focused on the street where the group hid. James felt his heartbeat slow as it continued to search. It took the first step forward. The sound was thick and heavy, and the pavement cracked under its weight. With each step, it dragged its right arm which was longer than the left. Those knuckles left dark tracks on the pavement. Ethan shrank down even further.

"Alice," James whispered. "It's gonna find Ethan."

"No, it won't. Get down and crawl under the car."

While James did as he was told, Alice made eye contact with Roger and nodded. Then she moved from her hiding place, staying on the sidewalk out of sight of the creature. She passed Dale and gave her the sign to get down as far as she could. Dale followed James's suit and crawled under a broken-down car. Roger got on the sidewalk side of the car he was hiding against just as Alice made it to the corner. The creature was close enough to put his hand down on Ethan's head when Alice screamed.

Alice's face contorted with her scream, showing all of her teeth. The red haze in her eyes narrowed the world to her and the creature down the street. It screamed back in a thousand pained voices and broke into an unsteady run. With its distorted right arm, it lashed out at the objects in its way. James winced as the car above him shifted, smashed sideways by the impact of another car. Then it was past him as well. Dale only saw its misshapen feet as it ran past her. Once Dale was safe, Alice darted out of the street. It screamed at its escaping prey and chased her around the corner.

Roger, Ethan, and Dale emerged from their hiding places.

"Get off the street. That noise is going to attract problems."

"We can't leave Alice."

"Ethan, get James and let's go. She'll have to take care of herself." Roger said.

Ethan hesitated. Roger gave him a shove. "GO!"

James was already crawling out from under the car and when Ethan grabbed him did his best to help get off the ground. Ethan could barely lift him but with Roger's help, they managed to get him into the stairwell of a building nearby.

Just as they did, the first edge of the rain reached the city. It stained the streets a darker shade and hid the marks of them and the monster.

"Dale, building sweep. Start on this floor and move up. Don't open any doors."

"Yes, Dad." Dale snuck around the corner toward the first apartment.

With the sunlight gone, the interior of the staircase felt like a tomb. Roger's and Ethan's hurried breathing didn't help. It was as if they were all suffocating. James had a moment for a fond memory of being stuck in the Central freezer. At least then, there had been chocolate. Outside, thunder rumbled across the world muffling everything with its strength. Lightning flashed, seeming to strike in the street outside.

"Do you think she's lost it or killed it?" Ethan asked.

Roger didn't reply, but instead guided James to sit on the bottom stair and went back to the front door. He searched out into the rain.

"We're going to be staying here awhile. Go help Dale sweep the building. I don't want surprises," Roger said.

"Don't open any doors?" Ethan asked.

"No. Don't open any doors." Roger didn't react to the joke but kept looking out. Once Ethan was gone, he asked James," Have you two ever seen anything like that before?"

"Other than the one in the hydro-garden, no, so I don't think Alice has ever seen one."

"What are her chances of coming out alive?"

"My money is always on Alice. If you haven't noticed, she's not fragile," James said.

"But she can die," Roger said.

"She doesn't stay that way." James tried not to think about watching her take three bullets in the chest and fall.

Roger turned sharply as a light appeared on the staircase above them. A candle held by a woman who peered over the staircase railing at them.

"What's all the commotion?" she asked, shining the light down toward them. Her night gown hung to her ankles and looked well-worn. Her hair, graying at the temples was bound back in a long braid. Her eyes were nearly as gray as her hair. "Mr. Anders?"

"I don't know a Mr. Anders," Roger said. Behind the staircase, Dale and Ethan had finished sweeping the floor of problems. He gave them a stay put signal with one hand. "We just came to take shelter here for a little while."

"Was that the Walker I heard out there?"

"The Walker?"

"Big hulking thing, likes to throw cars, drags one arm. Screams sometimes." Her description almost seemed calm, but her free hand twisted the hem of her nightgown hard.

"Yeah, that was it," Roger said.

"Hiding from it, huh?" It was a question, but she kept going as if it wasn't. "Might as well come on up. Don't see much of other folks, so company's appreciated. I'm Beatrice." With that, she turned around and headed back up the stairs.

Ethan chose to stay down by the front door and watch for Alice while the others went upstairs.

Beatrice lived on the third floor in an apartment not much bigger than a breadbox. One bedroom, a tiny kitchen, an even smaller bathroom, and a living room all decorated in various shades of deep brown, gold, and rust. It was a fall colored home which brought to mind Thanksgiving and turkey and togetherness. Roger and Dale struggled to get James up the stairs and were more than happy to drop him on the floor where he could make his own way up to sitting on the couch. He collapsed back into the cushions with a sigh.

"Why are you dragging him about?" Beatrice asked going into her kitchen. She returned and put a small gas stove on the coffee table.

"Are you talking about me?" James asked.

"I am."

"Usually I have a friend who carries me."

"A friend with eyes like yours?" She lit the stove with a long match and then blew it out slow.

James sat forward at those words. Dale, who had been looking out the window at the rain, turned to look at her as well.

"How did you know?" James asked.

"Oh, don't take offense now," she said, putting an old silver teapot on the stove. "Was just something I heard. Word comes slow these days, but sometimes, it still comes."

"What have you heard?"

Beatrice sighed. "Will you tell me about where you're coming from if I tell you?"

Roger agreed to the bargain, though James shook his head no.

"Well, a man, traveling into town from the west stopped here much the same way you did, hiding from the Walker. It don't care nothing for no one. Even the murders don't come too close to it. You'll find around here is fair quiet and only gets quieter when it's about."

James peered into her face, lit as it was from the fire of the stove. Her eyes were still too gray. Too blank.

"I offered him my hospitality in return for company, and he asked me if I knew about the ones with the strange eyes.

At first, he thought I might be one, but once he'd looked at me good, he decided it couldn't be me." The pot started to cry in pain. "He said, I ought to be wary of the ones with the mismatched eyes. A man with no legs and a dead woman carrying him. If you see them, know well that what brought this evil wants them. The *One from the Trench* wants their lives to complete his own."

"The *One from the Trench*?" Dale changed seats to sit beside James who had sat back and closed his eyes like a man with a headache.

"I don't know what it means. I just know he says it's in the East, waiting. And near it is dangerous. Best to stay away."

"We can't," James said. "We have to go East."

"You go East, you go toward your death, young man. Know that well." Beatrice warned.

"Staying here isn't actually safer, you realize?" Dale had wrapped an arm around James's shoulders.

"Where is Alice?" James asked.

"She'll be here," Dale reassured him.

The woman poured tea into a few cups.

Ethan and Alice came up the stairs as the woman placed the teacups into Roger and Dale's hands. James pushed his away. When Alice entered, he put his arms out to her, waiting for her to come to him and hug him.

"You worry me when you go away," he said.

"I'm fine." Alice turned around to demonstrate.

"Did you kill it?" James asked.

"No."

Alice sat down on the floor in front of James's legs.

"I didn't want to take the time, so I simply got far enough ahead and doubled back."

"Good plan."

Beatrice stared at them with big eyes and an even bigger mouth. "He described you, but I never thought I would see you."

Alice reacted to the stare with a tightening of her lips and her own stare.

"Please, take no offense. I just..."

"Alice, she says there's something in the East waiting for us," James said.

"Not waiting, drawing," Roger said. "It makes sense. If it wants you or needs you, then getting you to where it is would be important. Whatever is in the East is calling you. Summoning you for its own ends."

Ethan made the sign for time out before saying, "Woah! What did I miss?"

Alice seemed less interested. She and James shared one of their quiet moments until he shook his head and spread his hands in confusion.

"Beatrice here says the word coming out of the East is that there is something called the *One From the Trench*. It is waiting in the East and it's looking for a dead woman and the crippled man she carries," Roger explained.

"I'm not dead," Alice remarked.

"Not at the moment." James smiled as though it were a joke. Alice shot him an angry look.

"I can't tell you any more than I know. I know the Walker is out there in the rain and will kill anything it can catch. Mr. Anders, who lived downstairs, went out a couple days ago and never came back. Folks sometimes stop here by accident and they give me some news. So, I've told you my news. Tell me yours."

The others fell silent as Roger told the story of how Central had risen and fallen. By the time he finished, the rain had slacked. Ethan and James napped. Alice sat cross-legged on the floor and watched the two talk. Dale had gone to the window and curled up there to watch the rain. As the tale wound to a close with them finding shelter in the staircase from the Walker, Alice asked, "The *One From the Trench*, what is it?"

Beatrice blinked in surprise at the sudden question.

"He didn't say. Only that it was evil, and it was best to get as far away from it as possible."

Silence lapsed.

"What are you thinking, Alice?" asked Roger.

"We can't verify the truth of her news," Alice said.

"I'm sorry?" Beatrice questioned.

"As you say, take no offense, but how do we know you're telling the truth?"

"What reason do I have to lie?" Beatrice asked, and sipped her tea.

"I don't know, and I don't know about the man who brought you the news. I only know I feel the pull to go East. Therefore, I will continue with what I know," Alice said.

"Perhaps I can convince you." Beatrice gathered herself up from her seat. "Come with me." She picked up the candle and lit it again with deft motions. "He told me one other thing and I know the truth of it."

She led Roger and Alice down the stairs, back to the front door. She paused there, listening through the wood for a moment before she opened the door and pointed to a sigil painted on the door. A crude medallion drawn on the wood. "He told me to paint this on my door. Once it was there, I would be safe from the zombies coming in. They would never cross the seal."

A round medallion with a pair of almond shaped eyes staring out of it. They were human in shape, but even without the mild suggestion of an inhuman mouth below them, the sense of inhumanness was strong. Alice shook her head. Roger stared a few beats longer.

"We need to go." Roger gestured.

"It's dark," Beatrice said.

"We need to go now," he insisted. "I'm going upstairs to get the others. We'll find another place to stay the night."

"Really, you can't stay?" Beatrice asked.

"No. I don't know what you've made a pact with by putting that on your door, but I'm certain I don't want to find out either." Roger yelled for Dale as he headed up the stairs, Alice only steps behind.

Dale was already gathering gear. James shook Ethan who had started to snore. The apartment formerly cozy and small had become coffin-like and suffocating.

"We're out of here."

Ethan stood up abruptly only to land back on the couch when his legs gave out from under him.

"Coming," Ethan mumbled.

Alice hefted James who formed silent questions that she refused to answer. Beatrice stood in the doorway as they gathered everything.

"Thank you for everything," Roger said, "but we'll be going."

She stepped aside and waved them out.

"Was so pleasant to have you. Be careful wherever it is you go."

They trooped down the stairs into the dark. Together, they crossed four streets before hearing the Walker making its rounds of the neighborhood. They ducked into what had once been a pay by the hour motel. Dirty, foul smelling, but blessedly free of infestation, at least on the second floor where they took up residence. The group didn't bother sweeping the entire building, just the one floor. Anything that could have gotten further down was already out. Anything further up was more than likely trapped for good. They slept on gathered bedclothes from several different rooms and took up only one.

Alice laid down on the floor and folded her hands corpse-like over her chest. James lay much the same. At least until the dream started again.

He was once more on a rainy highway, his bike beneath him thrumming its counterpoint to the song in his head. James knew he wasn't going to die, but fear of the coming pain rose in his mind.

Take me down to the river.

The dream wasn't the same. A little girl appeared in the middle of the road. She said something. Through the driving rain, the song on his lips, the thrum of his bike, he couldn't make it out. Her lips moved. She repeated herself. Once. Then twice.

Wake up, Uncle.

The bike went through her without slowing and began to fall. He was falling. He was going to hit. He hit. Skidded. Now he heard her clearly screaming.

"Wake up, Uncle!"

The words came out of James's mouth in a flood as he bolted up to a sitting position. In the dark, the eyes of his companions glittered like predators and he shivered before starting to cry.

"Wake up, uncle," he repeated. He dropped back into the lying position, staring up at the ceiling. The tiles were discolored, water damage probably. Rolling over, he looked at Alice who had opened her eyes but not moved from the floor. Then he blinked, seeing the girl and the woman in the same moment. Was the girl Alice? But he couldn't be her uncle? Could he? That would just be weird. He pillowed his head on his arm and continued to stare.

The girl in the dream. He made himself concentrate on her. A little girl, maybe 7 or 8, wearing a dark blue school jumper and a white shirt. The white shirt had a red stain above her heart. Her eyes were big, frightened big. Warm brown skin. Dark brown, black hair pulled back in a ponytail. His mind flickered back to her eyes. Again, he saw Alice's face and the little girl's in the same glance. The mismatched eyes. One hazel, the other green.

"Take me on down to the river," James sung softly.

"The place where I was born." Alice added. She had closed her eyes again. "Go back to sleep, James." The others had already apparently done so.

"What river, Alice?"

"I don't know. Maybe it's in the East too. Now go back to sleep."

James didn't go back to sleep. Instead, he pondered the little girl who looked too much like Alice not to be Alice.

Morning set them back on the road headed toward the I-11 exit. Roger couldn't help noticing as they got closer the number of buildings where the medallion was painted on the door.

"That guy Beatrice talked to must have stopped a lot of places," he muttered.

"And that could mean something very bad," Alice offered, then started jogging jouncing James up and down on her back. The others started to trot to keep up.

The road rose and James knew without looking they were headed for a bridge. They were going to have to cross it to get out of town. Unfortunately, it was mostly missing. The support structure on the edges continued to hold, but the center had collapsed into the river below to become a flotilla of concrete.

"What do you think did that?" Ethan asked after whistling appreciatively at the destruction.

"Explosives," Roger said quickly scanning the edges. "We should be able to crawl the sides so long as we hold on tight."

"Take me down to the river," James said, his eyes fastened on the fast-moving water below.

"I don't think down is really an option here, James," Dale said.

Alice nodded in agreement, but her expression was a grimace of concentration.

"It might be the only option, if those sides aren't as secure as I think they are. The last thing we want to do is find out halfway across that we're hanging out in midair with no way forward or back." Roger's assessment was quick and thorough. "Alice, how much do you and James weigh together?"

"I don't know."

"Guess."

"350, maybe four hundred pounds all together."

"I'm worried what's left won't hold both of you and there is no way we can set James down to work himself across. I can already see there are going to be places we basically have to tightrope." Roger went to the edge of the bridge still settled on the ground and looked down into the hole. Ethan joined him.

"If we try to skip across the river on those rocks, we're running the risk of the water snatching us."

"Probably still better than falling on those rocks from above." Roger waved for Dale. "You're the lightest, want to go first?"

"Want? No. Will? Yes."

The gray pillar which had once been a mainstay of the bridge, called the Tener for the fact it was a legitimate extension of Tenth Street, was now crumbling around the edges.

"How are we going to get the packs down?"

"Drop it. Whatever breaks is broken."

Dale did exactly that. The backpack hit the ground with a *thud*, and she started down the side. Free climbing down the side of a pillar losing sections like an overly dry cake was a slow process. The others watched as she made her way down. Once she was clear, Ethan went down next.

Roger next.

When it was just Alice and James, Alice climbed down with James still attached to her back. A section of the pillar gave under her hands, turning her loose in the air. She landed on her feet, but it was a moment before she moved as if she had broken something and was afraid to make it worse with movement.

"You okay?" asked Roger.

"The light is fleeing," Alice said by way of response.

Alice was right. The day wore on and staying right there with the river overnight didn't seem the brightest idea.

"Dale," Roger said.

She shouldered her pack and started picking her way across.

"This would be one of those moments when I really wish we hadn't ditched the rope," Ethan said.

"Too bad. We've got to make some time here, kids," Roger said.

Each of them jumped behind the person in front working their way across. Ethan made the third jump and slipped, sliding into the water. Roger jumped too and grabbed hold, only to have the combined weight of Ethan and the water drag him in as well. He managed to get Ethan pushed back up on the concrete, but his own weight was too much. The river snatched him from the young man's grip and engulfed him.

"Roger!" Dale screamed from the far bank as Ethan hastily shoved his pack away and slid into the water after his friend.

Alice made it to the far side with James and stopped, looking back, then toward the embankment they would have to climb to get back on the road.

James said, "We can't leave him."

Dale worked her way back to where Ethan half hung in the water, one hand out to Roger gripping a rock just out of arm's reach. The water pushed Roger even further away where he grabbed on again, choking against the spray.

Alice turned her head to make eye contact with James before shrugging.

"Down."

He got down without protest.

Alice skipped across the distance, moving from one piece of nearly submerged concrete to another. When she reached Ethan and Dale trying to form a human chain, she waded in, putting one hand back for Ethan to grab hold. They still weren't long enough. Then Alice let go. The force of the water slammed her into Roger and they both tumbled under.

Ethan pulled back, looking at the place they had been. Dale wrapped her arms around her shoulders and buried her face in his neck. He patted her arm, but his eyes never left the river. No heads. The water had to be keeping them under. No heads.

Then dark hair broke the surface. Alice's black dreads hung heavy around her face as she emerged from the deep, one of Roger's arms around her neck. They'd been swept down river a hundred yards, but she crawled up onto the bank and laid Roger on the packed dirt.

Roger coughed, spit, and turned over on his side. His pack was gone. Victim of the river, but he wasn't.

"Thank you, Alice," he gasped.

She looked from him to James who only smiled. Alice picked Roger up and carried him back to James and the group was together again.

"I think we should take a break. Find a space and dry out," Ethan said.

Roger nodded his agreement.

They found a rest area not far off the bridge and though the sun was not yet setting, they settled for the night.

CHAPTER FIFTEEN

Dale versus Alice

"YOU WOULD HAVE LEFT HIM," DALE SAID.

"Yes," Alice's response was quiet.

She was looking out at the road, staring at it in fact, as if the asphalt would somehow change or spit out something they hadn't already seen. On this side of the river, they hadn't seen any zombies, not yet. Maybe there weren't any. Maybe they were all trapped in the maze of the city looking for those who hadn't had the guts to make for the country where the elements might kill them just as easily as the zombies.

Roger, the subject of their conversation, lay only a few feet away covered with a blanket. His clothes hung from the edge of the counter, dry now after a few hours of hanging there. James and Ethan had both fallen asleep nearby, though James occasionally rolled and moaned something neither of them could quite catch. Alice would look at him, when he spoke, her own face uncertain.

"Why?"

"East."

"I know that already. There is something in the East. Something there that might have the answer to all this. Or might not." Dale spread her hands out as if to say give her more.

"Yes."

"I don't understand."

"I need to go East. I nearly left James the last time he slowed me down. The need is..." Alice paused and shook her head.

James broke the silence when he called out to her in his sleep. He fought his way up out of his dream, opening his eyes. Alice wrapped her arms around him and drew his head to her chest, cradling him there. Closing her eyes, she rocked him gently.

"And he is all I have." Alice added.

Dale watched it happen. Watched and tried to understand.

Alice fought the pull to wait for them.

"Alice?"

"Yes?"

"Will you leave him behind?"

"I don't know."

When she rose, Alice picked James up with her, cradling him against her body like a doll.

"Maybe," she said. "I have nothing."

With that, Alice walked away from Dale, leaving her to watch over Ethan and Roger while she relocated James to a picnic table. Then Alice laid down next to him, taking on her posture of the newly dead.

Roger coughed. Dale checked his temperature. He wasn't hot, but there was no telling what morning would be like.

Morning dawned gray, the world still shrouded in clouds. Another storm gathered in the distance. Dale woke up to find Alice sitting on her haunches once again with her eyes on the road.

"It's not going to move," Dale said.

Alice looked at her then shook her head. James sat close by, but he kept mum on the subject. At least until Ethan joined them.

"We may have a problem," Ethan said.

"What?" James piped up.

"I think Roger's taking sick. He's in the bathroom right now puking into one of the toilets, so I figured I'd tell you guys first," Ethan said with a sigh.

"We can't leave him," Dale said.

James scooted closer to Alice and grabbed her arm, tugging on it like a toddler looking for attention. She leaned down and kissed him on the forehead.

When Roger joined them, silence fell so fast he turned in place.

"Did something happen?" he asked.

"We're just worried about you," Dale said.

"I was a little sick, but I'm fine. We should get going." Roger gave them a weak smile, but he coughed again, covering his mouth. He replaced his smile and started marching.

"Hey, if we're going to keep going, you should be carrying some of the groceries," Ethan said.

James hung onto Alice, holding her back from following Roger.

"Alice, we can't leave them," James said.

"I don't want to, but we can't let them stop us either." Then she slung him up on her back and started walking. James put his head against her neck and settled for the ride.

"She was going to leave him," Dale said.

"Dale, you don't know that," Ethan replied.

"I do know that. I asked her. She was going to walk away and leave Roger to drown. Do you understand? She doesn't care about any of us. All that matters to her is getting East."

"But she helped us against the Walker, Dale. If she was just going to abandon us, then she could have just let that thing kill us."

"I know." Dale made a face. "All I'm saying is that we can't trust she's going to help all the time. What happens when she decides her goal is more important than our lives?"

"We fight for our lives," Roger added. "You two aren't exactly quiet. In fact, I'm pretty sure she can probably hear you. So, let's get one thing straight. We're going to keep going East toward Senora. If we get a chance, maybe we'll stop before we get there. If it will keep us alive."

"So, you're saying we abandon them?"

"Yes. If it comes to that, that's exactly what we're going to do," Roger said.

CHAPTER SIXTEEN

Those of the Trench

EVERY DAY THEY ROSE AND WALKED. EVERY day, they slept where they found a safe space. Zombies were fewer, thankfully, but the elements were more dangerous. Bridges crumbled. Sections of the highway had slid into holes full of soft ground. They found their way around those places as best they could. And every morning, Alice would be found sitting, staring at the road ahead.

Yet she stayed with them, keeping their pace.

At midday perhaps two weeks later, the group was forced to seek shelter when another storm, this one laced heavily with lightning, blew up out of the East. It seemed to be trying to drive them West, which it did, off the highway and into what could have once been considered a picturesque little town. The rain drove them like cattle down the main street, above the single stoplight swung back and forth in the wind like a clapper-less bell. As the wind slung rain at them, they found themselves on the steps of a building which from the columns was either a bank or city hall. Whatever it was, they threw themselves up the stairs and through the doors, struggling to shut them behind them.

The doors shut with an echoing clang.

Dale slumped to the floor, her dark hair streaming water into her eyes. Shaking her head, she tried to clear her vision.

Beyond the doors, the room was shrouded in darkness. Dale strained to see what might be there. Nearby, she could hear James scooting along the tile floor.

"Nothing there," he said as he laid down on his stomach next to her. "Just a lot of dark and some old furniture."

"Thanks."

"No charge."

"Ethan and I are going to scout the rest of what's here. No need to set ourselves up for surprises."

"There won't be any."

Alice stood in the doorway looking out at the rain. Then she tapped the doors themselves. In their haste, no one had noticed the sign on the door.

The eyes stared back from the glass untouched by the driving rain. Not smeared as they had been other places, they passed through but deliberately painted.

"I don't like the look of that," said Roger.

"I'm thinking as soon as the weather clears..."

"We're getting out of here. But until it does, we might as well work on getting dry and fed," Roger said.

The storm raged, pinning them down for the night. As the others laid down, Alice sat, looking at the door. Dale joined her, drawing her knees up to her chest. The rain battered on, but that was the only sound.

"You want to go on despite the rain," Dale said.

"Yes." For a moment, Alice said nothing. "James has been sleeping badly."

"You noticed?"

"Yes. He dreams of an accident he doesn't remember having. And a little girl in a blue jumper that he thinks might be me. Except it can't be me. I'm not a little girl and there's no wound over my heart." She shook her hair out and then combed her fingers through the dreads to straighten them. "He's afraid."

"I know, he told me," Dale said.

Alice nodded in agreement.

James sat against a wall braiding strips of an old shirt into rope. It kept his hands busy and usually as long as his hands were busy, his mouth was shut. A win-win for everyone.

"Is he dreaming or remembering?" Alice asked.

"I don't know," Dale said, spreading her hands in a gesture of defeat. "I wish I did."

"Watch over him." With slow motions, Alice reached up and took the necklace from around her neck and put it in Dale's hands.

Dale looked up as Alice unfolded herself to her full height, stretched toward the ceiling, took one glance back at the others, and let herself out into the rain. The door hung open, letting a spray of water in on the tiles.

"Hey wait!" Dale shouted.

Alice disappeared into the elements.

When Dale looked back, she could see James staring at the door Alice had used. His eyes were large, his mouth hung open in a soundless scream. Then he pressed his hands to his face. Dale ran over, dropped down beside him, and wrapped her arms around his shaking shoulders.

"It's okay," Dale hugged him close.

"She left me."

"She'll be back."

"She told you to watch over me. She's not coming back." James folded even smaller, deflating against Alice's abandonment.

Ethan shut the door and the rain returned to beating against it with its monstrous ferocity. Roger coughed from where he sat.

"We're going to have to figure out how we're going to manage to keep moving without her to carry him," Ethan said to Roger as he resumed his seat. "Otherwise, we won't have any choice but to leave him too."

"Or we could just stay here. It's an empty town. We set up shop here," Roger said.

"No, we've got to keep going to Senora," Ethan said.

"Ethan, we can't manage without her. The best we can hope to do is get ourselves killed."

"We still need to find answers, Roger. We aren't going to find them hiding out here."

"We're not going to find them if we're dead either."

"Stop it!" Dale still held the slowly rocking James. "We can't go anywhere in this rain. So, chill out. James, it's gonna be okay."

"There's something out there in the rain." James lifted his head to the door. "There's something in the rain...looking..."

He twisted out of Dale's grip and crawled toward the door. "Looking for us."

Dale followed him. Outside, the rain sheeted, but it was light enough now to see objects across the road. He pressed his face against the glass.

Across the road, untouched by the rain, was a girl no more than eight years old. Her hair hung in thick strands which fell past her shoulders. The dark blue of her jumper appeared black in the low light, but the red of her heart wound pulsed with a scarlet light. Above it, her eyes stood out in sharp relief, bright to the point of dominating her face. James could see her mouthing words.

"Help me, uncle," he said slowly. "How?" The question came out involuntarily.

"James, is that her?" Dale asked.

"Yeah. How do I help you? Who are you?" James shouted. She mouthed another word.

"Alice. But what about Alice?" He shook his head and pressed his face against the glass so hard his nose began to bleed.

"I am Alice." He repeated after the phantom. Then in a flash of lightning, the little girl was gone and what stood in her place was a monster they had seen before, its stitched together flesh soaked through and eyes rolling in its sockets.

"Get away from the door!" James warned.

It came barreling toward them.

James dropped flat, covering his head with his hands as it came through the glass. The metal of the door twisted with a human shriek, which James added to when it stepped on his lower back, smashing him into the floor. Dale had thrown herself to one side, and barely missed losing part of her face to the flying glass.

It snapped a column in the center of the room with its weight. Luckily, neither Roger nor Ethan had stayed anywhere near it. They found positions on the edge of the room.

"Wait for it to turn," Roger called.

Memories of the cistern came back to him. The luminescent eyes. The weak spot. The Walker turned toward Ethan with a roar, slowing only enough to realize it had prey before it. It swept out with its oversized right arm just as Ethan fired. The bullets buried themselves in its flesh and it advanced, another scream tearing from its throat.

"Ethan!" Dale uncurled from her place by the door, yelling, and the monster turned again, now toward Dale.

Her face fell as it ran toward her. Both Ethan and Roger fired, and it didn't even slow. It thrust its massive right hand forward to grab and just as it did, James snatched Dale out from under it. Overbalanced, it rolled forward.

"Go!" James yelled as the thing tumbled down the steps. Instead of doing as she was told, Dale grabbed him by the arm to drag him out of harm's way. He shook her off.

"Get!" he repeated.

It was coming back. A flash of lightning turned it into a hulking shadow in the doorway and the rumble of thunder almost covered the sound of its footsteps as it moved more cautiously now, as though it were unsure of where exactly they were. Ethan scrapped his foot along the tile to get a better position and it swung its head toward him before letting loose another deafening scream. Ethan brought his gun up and let it close its mouth before he neatly put two bullets in its eye sockets.

The fall would have made an elephant carcass proud.

Dale covered her mouth with both hands as the thing came apart, the places where its flesh held together loosening and an ooze slipping out.

"Help." James put his arms up. Ethan slung his weapon back and dragged him away from the mess. Before long, the body was little more than a slimy puddle mixing with rainwater.

"Was that thing the little girl you saw?" Ethan asked.

"No. Yes. I don't think so." James's answers all came out in a tumble. His tongue tripped over itself to make what his brain didn't understand verbal. "I don't know. She..." He stopped and buried his face in his hands to take a deep breath. "She said she was Alice, and Alice isn't one of those things."

"But we also don't know what Alice is, or what you are for that matter," Roger said before settling on the floor. "We need to find a way to block that door."

Ethan watched the rain for a long breath before continuing.

"That thing shouldn't have been able to come across the threshold."

"Unless what Beatrice said was a lie," James said. "After all, we only had her word."

"Doesn't matter. We need to either block or get away from that door. Anything out there could come looking any second." Roger put one hand under James's arm and let Ethan get the other side. "Dale. Find us somewhere to go."

"Going," she said.

They spent the night, all four of them, in the remains of a break room with a window the size of a postage stamp and a former soda machine dropped in front of the door.

The next morning was still dark. Clouds threatened but delivered no rain.

"We need to get going," Roger said.

James sat on the floor, his eyes on the destroyed door and avoiding the greasy space of rotten flesh left behind by the Walker.

"You'll have to leave me behind," he said.

"We're not leaving you, you idiot," Dale said, wrapping her arm around his shoulders.

"Roger can't carry me. Ethan can't carry me. You sure as hell can't carry me, Chipmunk. If someone can't carry me, I can't go," James said.

"We'll find a way." She pressed her head to his face.

"Don't worry about finding a way. Find the truth." He hid his face and pushed her away. "Find Alice."

"We're not leaving you. Roger, tell him."

"Dale, he's right," Ethan said.

"Ethan?"

"Dale."

"See?" James pushed her again, forcing space between them. "Just go."

"We can't leave him here." Dale glared.

Neither Roger nor Ethan responded as Dale got up.

"We are not leaving him."

"Then you stay here with him," Roger said.

Dale physically recoiled from Roger's voice, stepping away from James as she did.

"We aren't going to leave him." Then she looked down at James. "And nothing you say is going to make us leave you."

The sound of footsteps startled them out of their argument. Everyone brought their weapons up and turned toward the sound. A man was coming up the city hall steps, his hands out in front of him in a gesture of peace.

"Hello?" he said.

Roger waved them to lower their weapons.

"Hello," Roger said.

"I..."

Ethan took a step forward, slinging his weapon backward to let it settle on his back.

"Dad?" Ethan frowned.

"Ethan?" Surprise lit up both of their faces and then Ethan stumbled into a run and threw his arms around the older man.

"I thought you were dead."

Dale settled back on the floor next to James and wrapped her arms around his shoulders.

"I almost was, but..." Christopher Post looked at the group with wide eyes. "I managed to make it through. I left you in the city. I wanted you to be safe."

"The city wasn't safe, Dad, you knew that when you left." Ethan stepped back, putting the man at arm's reach. "Now." Ethan shook his head rather than finish the sentence. "Shit, I'm being rude. Those are Roger, Dale, and James."

"You pick some strange traveling companions, son." Christopher pushed back his hat. "And it looks like you've got a problem. Seeing as one of your friends has got no legs."

"Wow, observant of you," James said before Dale clapped her hand over his mouth. He said something else that came out muffled while giving Dale a rather nasty look.

"Don't mind him, his mouth has long since run away with his brain," she said with a smile.

"I remember a boy who used to be something like that," Christopher said with a chuckle looking at his son.

"He can still be something like that," Roger said before stepping past Christopher to look at the deserted street. "So, what are you doing here?"

"There was a commotion last night. Then this morning, the Walker wasn't where it normally was, figured I would come take a look around."

"Are there other people here?" Roger asked.

"Yeah. Hiding out. The Walkers aren't exactly friendly." He heaved a sigh and shook his head. "We're going to want to get moving. Before one of the others finds out this territory is up for grabs now."

"What do you mean?" Ethan asked.

"Walkers walk their territory constantly. When they come upon each other, let's just say World War II starts to look like a school yard brawl. One of them is going to want this space and it'll kill everything to get it."

"If you're not going to leave me, Ethan's going to have to carry me." James put his arms up like a toddler wanting to be held.

"Might be easier if we get him a wheelchair," Christopher said. "There's a hospital in town."

Roger raised an eyebrow.

"Could take you to get it, Ethan, leave your friends to hold down the fort," Christopher said.

"Why two people?" asked Dale.

"Always at least one weapon," Roger said. When he turned to Ethan, he shrugged. "Your call, kid."

"Actually, it's your call, Roger. You're in charge," Ethan said.

"Then go. Get a wheelchair. Anything that will make this easier. Me and Dale will hold down the fort here, move back into the break room for the duration."

"Good enough for me. Let's go, E." Christopher said.

Ethan smiled.

Christopher led the way off the stairs with Ethan following. Roger looked down at Dale.

"I don't know that I like this," Roger said.

"Ethan's dad," Dale whispered.

"Yeah. Good for him, but..." Roger didn't have to say that finding one family member only made him miss his own. His wife. Beautiful in her own uncertain simple way. His son. So young. Both of them so dead. Dale had been an orphan before this started. James had no memory, therefore no one to miss, except Alice.

"Let's move back into the break room. No use in making a spectacle of ourselves."

The town was quiet except for the sound of Christopher and Ethan Post walking. They stayed on the sidewalk, hugging the buildings.

"Dad, I..."

"Ethan, I left you to keep you safe. I was going to come back for you, once I was sure of things."

"Sure of things?" Ethan stomped along two steps behind his father. "You left me in a warzone, alone. I missed you. I thought you were dead."

"You said that already." Christopher shook his head and smiled. "I'd forgotten how strong you are. Forgotten how much like your mother you are."

Ethan's mother, buried as she was, had been a strong woman. One of those Take it or Leave it types who managed to marry well and raise a family without losing too much of their bark. She would have survived in spite of everything, if it hadn't been her little girl who got her. Miranda Post would have been shooting zombies and screaming obscenities the entire time.

The thought made Ethan smile.

"The hospital isn't that far." They turned onto a side street veering northward. Ethan could already see a building standing slightly higher than the others with all the earmarks of a corporate structure. As if every hospital in the world had something similar about it that marked it for what it was.

The Emergency Room doors were jammed shut with gurneys, but they managed to make a hole large enough to slide through, each of them crawling on their hands and knees. Inside was a Jackson Pollack of blood, entrails, limbs, and heads; bodies torn apart and strewn like doll pieces in a shop. Ethan tried not to think about the lives those bodies had previously lived. Instead, he scanned the area for what they had come for: a wheelchair.

They found one in an exam room where the floor had been repainted with the contents of a human circulatory system. Together, Christopher and Ethan cleaned the wheels so they could push it out.

"We'll need to find another way out."

Rather than use the Emergency Room exit, they headed for the main entrance of the hospital. Ethan kept his eyes on the wheelchair rather than looking around. The front doors of the hospital were less cluttered, but only because it seemed as if they had been used in the exodus. The doors themselves hung skewed from their hinges, broken by the flood of escaping bodies.

As they entered the front lobby, the sound of something large moving came to them with a steady *thud*.

"Walker." Christopher gestured to stop and stay down with one hand while he drew the wheelchair to a stop.

"Shit." Ethan got down.

"Just wait. We'll let it pass. We should be fine."

The sound of the creature running made them both drop flat. Outside the hospital doors, a Walker sprinted past and disappeared from sight. Ethan held his breath against the fear in his chest and the smell now plastered across his face.

Long seconds passed as the footsteps retreated. When Ethan lifted his face from the floor, Christopher was already on his knees, looking at the broken doors. Christopher breathed hard as if he'd been running.

"Is it gone?" Ethan asked.

"I think so. We should go."

"But what was it chasing?"

"I don't know. Whatever it was, best to get out of this territory, now. Let's get going," Christopher said.

The pair walked through the hospital doors and back onto the street, each footstep slow and light. They had cleaned the wheels of the chair so that it didn't squeak, something Ethan was thankful for. Christopher pushed the wheelchair down the sidewalk with Ethan close behind.

"It will come back, won't it?" Ethan asked.

"Yes, probably. So, let's get off the street."

A forgotten soda can popped out of the gutter as the wind rose, clattering as it went. Another storm rose, bringing new rain. At least the smell of coming rain helped drive away the gross scent already in Ethan's nose. They made the trip back to city hall double-time and as expected the front room was empty. Ethan charged in and called for Roger and Dale.

Roger poked his head out of the break room and was followed by Dale.

"Welcome back. Did you have fun?" Dale asked.

"Not really. There's a Walker out there. If we're going to get moving, we should get going," Ethan said.

"Where are you going?" Christopher asked.

Dale and Roger helped James into the wheelchair as Ethan turned to face his Dad.

"We've got to go to Senora, Dad. It's a small town up north," Ethan said.

"Is that a safe haven? I haven't heard about it." Christopher asked.

"No." Ethan shook his head. "Just trust me, Dad. We've got to go there."

"Ethan." Christopher's voice dropped as he said his son's name. "I'd rather you stayed here with me."

"Dad."

"We can at least stay the night. You can show us this group you've been living with," Roger said.

Both Posts looked at him; Ethan with gratitude, Christopher with fear.

"I'm hungry, so I hope there's food." James piped up.

"You're always hungry," Dale said.

"True, but that doesn't make it less important," James said.

"James, shut up," Ethan said.

"Did you miss saying that to me?" James grinned.

"No, not really, but thanks for the refresher." Ethan crossed his arms over his chest.

"Let's go." Dale sounded almost chipper from where she stood behind James's brand new, to him, wheelchair. "James is hungry and we're standing out in the open with our pants down right now."

"You always want to talk about the strangest stuff."

"Yep." James and Dale exchanged a high five.

"Like your friend says, we really ought to go." Christopher's smile was back in place and he looped one arm around his son's shoulders.

It took Ethan and Christopher to help guide-carry James down the City Hall steps, but once they were on the blacktop, it was smooth sailing. Christopher led them to what had once been a school. Now the school stood, deserted looking in the daylight, the former basketball court empty and silent. Its squat form, taupe walls, and mostly boarded up windows were hardly inviting. Christopher led them through a side door where they had to lift the wheelchair over the lip.

Inside the cafeteria, Christopher led the group through a door that emptied into a stale, cool, and fairly dark room. The skylights above had been darkened with paint as though to keep something from looking down into the building. The boarded windows showed warping from the rain. The wheelchair wheels made almost no sound on the floor as they made their way through the hallways and into the kitchen. In the kitchen was a fridge.

When he opened the door, James said, "Oh look, we're going to be meatsicles again. I wonder if there will be chocolate?"

Dale and Ethan both giggled as Roger rolled his eyes.

"Meatsicles?" Christopher asked.

"An inside joke, sorry," Ethan said, clapping his father on the shoulder. "I'll tell you all about it, later."

"I'm sure I'll love this story."

"Oh, it's hilarious. You just had to be there." Roger's tone said hilarious was the exact last thing he thought about their episode in the refrigerator back at Central. Christopher led them through the fridge and out the back, someone had opened it up and added a staircase leading down below the school.

"There used to be a way into the basement from inside the school, but it's mostly been blocked off. There was no way to reinforce the doors any further without making them impassable. While this door, nice and thick, but easy to open but they can't open it," he explained.

"I thought there weren't any zombies in this town."

"That wasn't always the case, I guess. By the time I got here, it was just the Walkers and they're bad enough. Though I've never heard of them going into a building."

"One crashed through the doors of the City Hall last night to visit us, so trust, they do go into buildings." Dale made a face at the memory.

ALICE

The words wandered back from the tight walls, only barely wide enough to allow James's wheelchair to go down. Ethan held it from tumbling down the stairs with James's help, inching down one stair at a time. The bottom of the stairs came quickly, thankfully. Ethan was sweating and panting.

"Man, that's heavy." Ethan wiped his face.

"This way." Christopher led them down a corridor lit by only the occasional small lantern. The sounds of others drifted toward them, including some laughter. What they entered at the first room was a school room. Several children sat staring at a board as a woman indicated something on it with a stick. Christopher kept moving, ushering them past quickly. He stopped in a room the size of an American living room, lit by lanterns hung overhead. Several people were there. They all appeared to be praying.

"I brought newcomers," Christopher said, stopping outside the praying circle. A man stood up and gestured for the others to remain where they were.

"Post. We wondered where it was you had gone. It's not safe to go above, you know that."

"I know, but after the storm..."

"Yes, the storm. Always the storms. You shouldn't have risked yourself." The man clasped his hands behind his back and stalked toward them, face pressed forward as if he would take a bite out of someone without getting any blood on his shirt. His white hair was plastered back against his skull except for one tuft over his left ear sticking out like an unsmoothed feather. "And who are these you've brought?"

James didn't pipe up first. In fact, there were several seconds of complete silence before Roger spoke.

"Roger Mackie." Roger didn't offer his hand. "And these folks are mine. Dale Bernard."

Dale cut a mock curtsy.

"Ethan Post."

Ethan didn't bow.

Not even when Christopher said, "My son, Ethan."

"And James Smith."

James bowed from where he was sitting.

"You've come from? "The Preacher Man stalked right up until he was breathing Roger's air. His eyes flickered across the lot of them like a man surveying cattle. Behind him, several of the prayer circle had risen to their feet.

Ethan sniffed. The underground was less stale and more rank. Like Central, though Central had been a sewer it had a similar smell, the unwashed human body packed in by the dozen. Though there was another smell, one he almost identified, then pushed away.

"That doesn't matter. We're here and none of us are infected."

"Papa." A woman old enough to be Dale's mother stepped up to the Preacher Man's elbow and nudged him lightly. "They traveled, so they are able. All but that one, and that should be enough."

"It is, Cecilia, but one cannot be sure in times like this. However, since Mr. Post has brought them to us, we should at least make them welcome."

His face cracked into a smile which it treated as an unwelcome and quickly shooed off guest.

"Please, let Mr. Post show you to some sleeping spaces. I'm sorry to say we won't be eating the noon meal today. Food's scarce, so it's concentrated for dinner time." He waved them back out of the room with one long hand. His nails were yellow and long, making his fingers claws-like.

They were most of the way down the next hall before Ethan pulled his father to a stop.

"Who was that guy?" Ethan jerked his thumb in the direction they'd come.

"He's called Papa by most of the people here. The oldest living resident and all that. He used to be a preacher, back when this was actually a town, I've heard. I don't know much more than that."

"Not a big fan of new people, is he?" Ethan asked.

"Nope. I've been here a while and he still isn't fond of me. Doesn't matter though." Christopher Post smiled at his son. "You're here and this will become home all too soon."

"Sure, Dad." Ethan dropped back to walk beside James's wheelchair.

The sleeping spaces were nothing but rows of army cots in a what had once been a bomb shelter. The walls were more brown than gray now, but they were still obviously metal.

"You can stow your gear anywhere that doesn't look occupied. Those over there in the corner should do for you," Christopher said.

"How many people live here?" Dale asked.

"I'm not sure. Maybe 75, not a lot. Some of them are kids. You saw them."

Dale nodded.

"I'm still hungry," James said as he rolled up to the end of one of the cots, maneuvering the chair around as if he had spent time in one before.

"So, anything coming back to you?" Roger dropped down on the end of a cot and then flopped backward, arms over his head laying out long.

"Huh?" James shot him a confused expression.

"You, James, anything coming back to you? You drive that wheelchair like you've been in one for years," Roger said.

"No, nothing specific. But the little girl..."

Dale put her hand down on his shoulder and shook her head.

"What little girl?" Christopher asked.

"I thought I saw a little girl last night, that's all." James put the wheels in park and made the transfer onto the cot without help. "Nothing serious. Probably just the rain and my brain playing tricks."

"Hey, Dad, they have any cards in this place? I'm pretty sure I can still take you in Five-Card Draw," Ethan said, drawing the conversation away from James.

"You're on, kid." The Post pair walked out together.

Dale sat down on the end of James's cot and untied his shoes.

"I don't like that preacher guy." She stared after Ethan and his father.

"He doesn't seem like a terribly likable guy," said James.

"Well, it's a safe space. Out of the wind. We should consider sticking around," said Roger.

"You serious?"

"Yes. Alice is gone. We've got to face the facts. Whatever we run into out there is liable to kill us without her to help, so why go back out there? Besides, Ethan's got his Dad back. He's not going to want to leave." Roger shrugged.

"Ethan? There's no way he would want to stay here," Dale said.

"You'd be amazed at how what you want changes when you suddenly have someone to share it with," James said, lying back against the thin pillow.

"She'll come back," Dale said.

"Maybe."

Dale dropped James's shoes next to his cot and then slipped off her own before lying down next to him. Rolling over, James put his arm around her.

"Well, I'll just leave you two alone," Roger said.

"It's not like that," Dale said, sitting up.

James chuckled. "I'm going to lie here until dinner. You don't have to stay."

"I'm going to take a nap. Then maybe, I'll get up, but no sooner." Dale curled back against James's body and Roger walked out, leaving them alone just as he promised.

Chapter Seventeen

Those of the Trench II

WHEN ROGER RETURNED, ETHAN IN TOW, from a rather rousing game of Five Card Draw with Christopher Post, James's cot was empty, and his wheelchair gone.

"Where's James?" asked Ethan. "And Dale?"

"I don't know. I left them here together." Roger scratched his head and looked at the empty cot. There was nowhere for Dale to hide. Just rows of military cots lined up for those who would find their rest there. James, with his wheelchair, would have been easy to see. Neither were in sight.

"That's weird." Ethan searched the room too.

"Yeah, but let's not panic yet. They could just be off exploring together or something." Roger felt the panic he was telling Ethan not to have creeping up inside him. James and Dale might wander off, but this wouldn't be the place. At least, he didn't think they would get far here.

"Let's go look." Ethan suggested.

"No, let's just wait. They'll pop back up as soon as the dinner bell rings. You know James doesn't miss a meal."

Christopher Post walked in and looped an arm over his son's shoulders.

"Been a long while since you beat me that badly."

"Been a long while since we played, Dad." Ethan wrinkled his nose. "I think I'm ready for a nap."

"You sure?" Mr. Post asked.

"Yeah. We've been moving a lot lately. Gotta take rest when you can get it, right?" Ethan's smile went to Roger, where Roger could see the uncertainty creeping up in the boy's eyes.

For a moment, Roger remembered how young Ethan was and how young Dale was and how young James probably was. These kids, all in need of direction. They looked to him to provide it.

Ethan sat down on the cot next to where James's shoes lay. He looked down at the shoes, then back at Roger before nudging another small, Dale, shoe with his toe.

Roger's formerly baseless panic found a foundation.

"Well, I suppose I'll leave you to sleep. Roger, care for a grand tour of the place? It isn't much, but if you all are going to be staying here, then you might as well start learning your way around," Christopher said.

"That sounds like a good idea." Roger clapped Christopher on the back and turned him toward the door. Over his shoulder, he looked back to Ethan. "We won't be long." His eyes said, "Be on your guard".

As soon as they were out the door, Ethan stopped pulling off his shoes and got up. He watched the door for a moment as if waiting for something to come flying through it and take off his head, but nothing came. Then he walked to the other end of the room. It was a solid wall. Just metal showing signs of wear and constant interaction. A standard wall. Yet he couldn't shake the feeling of this place as a prison. Not a safe haven, though they were certainly safe, but rather a prison where everyone paid the price for their sins by being stuck there. He shut that thought away and walked back to the cot where Dale and James had been. Their shoes on the floor stared up at him. He leaned down and looked under the bed as though it were all just some huge joke and they would come bursting out to start laughing. There was nothing under the cot but those shoes.

"Where did you two go?" Ethan said aloud.

"Who?" He whirled to the sight of a woman standing in the doorway with a bundle of clothes held to her chest. "Where did who go?" She repeated her question.

"Two of my friends. We left them here to rest up and now they've taken off."

She smiled at him as she dropped the clothes down on a nearby cot with a *whumpf*. Then she picked up the clothes and started folding.

"Can't have gone far," she said. "There isn't much to our little paradise to wander in." Her face was down and her hands busy as she continued. "You're the new ones, the bunch everyone's talking about. The ones Post brought in."

"Yeah, my father brought us here," Ethan said.

Her head snapped up and she peered at him curiously then her smile brightened her face again.

"I see it. I do. Right there in your eyes. You're Christopher Post's boy. I bet he was glad to see you. We'd all be glad if someone we loved came back into our lives. What with all this danger and damage everywhere. But here is safe. Yes. Here is safe."

Her face slowly dropped again as she went back to folding her laundry.

"How long have you been here?" Ethan slid a little closer until he was at the far end of the cot from her.

"I can't rightly say," she said. "Seems like every day lasts a week down here. Papa doesn't like us going up onto the street unless we're looking for Walkers, and only a few get to do that. Those he trusts."

"Those he trusts?"

Ethan let that sink in.

"Yeah. Oh, I'm being dreadful rude. I'm Charlotte." She dropped her folding to lean across the cot and offer her hand. Ethan leaned forward to take her hand. It felt chill and thin and...

His bones crinkled as she tightened her grip.

"I'll take you to your friends."

She was still smiling but that smile was less perfect now, teeth yellowing and missing. Before his eyes, her own eyes melted, one of them turning sideways in the socket as if she had been hit with a bat at one time and it was never corrected. Charlotte jerked him toward her, and Ethan felt his shoulder pop.

"Yes, I will." Charlotte said.

He landed on his stomach, a tee-shirt dropping over his face. Her hand on the back of his head smashed his face into the cot until he couldn't breathe, only flail with his free hand. Charlotte said nothing else, holding until Ethan stopped fighting. By then, Papa was standing in the doorway, his hands clasped behind his crooked back.

"Well. Done."

Together, the pair lifted Ethan from the cot and carried him out of the room.

To say Roger listened to Christopher's tour might have been an overstatement. Truthfully, he was only really paying attention to where the possible exits were as they traveled through the underground complex. Oh, and where there were choke points which might be of use if they had to actually fight their way out. As much as Roger wanted to believe there was some chance this place was the safe haven he had envisioned them holding up in, he was certain something was going on he and he didn't really want to be a part of it. Time to take an exit, stage right.

The library, one of the few rooms borrowed wholesale from the school above, was overstocked. Every available surface had books on it, the shelves were packed to the point of nearly collapsing. Despite himself, Roger whistled in appreciation.

"That's a lot of books."

"I want to show you something." Christopher led the way through the stacks to a shelf which he scanned, his finger under every title, until he found the one he wanted and pulled it free. It came loose with a half dozen others dropping to the floor. Then he held it out to Roger.

"I knew I recognized you," Christopher said.

Roger looked at his own face on the dust jacket of *Rocking Chair Requiem: A Mystery Novel.*

"That was a long time ago," Roger said. He handed the book back. "Another lifetime ago."

"I thought you might like to see some part of that old life. That's what we're trying to make here, a little piece of the old life. Sure, everywhere is candles and lanterns now. We have to check our perimeter to go into the garden to get food, and there's always a good chance the sun might not come up tomorrow, but well, we're doing the best we can. Mankind is resilient and all that mess."

Christopher sat down in a nearby chair and leaned across a small table, probably made for children, and put the book down.

"A laudable goal." Roger sat down across from him. "Except I don't really think that's what you're trying to do here."

The two men eyed each other across the table until Christopher looked away.

"I want to thank you for everything you've done for my son. Keeping him safe, giving him someone to look up to. I made a huge mistake leaving him behind like that, but I thought he would be safe in Central, that everything would be okay until I could get back to him."

"Except you found this place and you got wrapped up in whatever is going on here, "Roger said.

"What do you mean?"

"Christopher. Mr. Post." Roger leaned back in his chair. "Two of my kids are missing out of your safe haven. Their shoes were right where they left them." Roger pushed the book across the table to his companion. "Want to tell me why?"

Christopher Post looked down at the face on the book jacket, then up at the man who looked as though he had aged a few years but still had a number of good years left in him. A man who might very well be willing to do something drastic for those he cared about. For a moment, Christopher's face contorted with fear, then shame.

"They aren't missing. They're taken," he said wearily. "The same way he's going to take Ethan and then you. You can't stay here if you don't let him, so I would suggest not fighting."

"Once you were here, you couldn't leave," Roger said.

"No. Once you're here, once you've been taken, you can't leave. Papa won't let you. It won't let you," Christopher said.

"It what?"

"The One of the Trench. The Monster. The Thing causing all this to happen." Christopher hid his face and when he showed it again, it was different.

His eyes formerly bright were now clouded and shivering in their sockets. The right side of his mouth drooped and split showing his teeth behind his smile. His skin, formerly healthy, now stood sallow and pocked. "You'll be like us."

Christopher crowded across the table at Roger, pushing it into Roger's legs. Unable to stand up, Roger still managed to get his hands up in time to ward off the blows Christopher rained on him.

"You should never have brought my son here," the former Christopher Post bellowed. "He was safe!"

Roger found himself with his book in his hands and it made a satisfying *pow* as it connected with Christopher Post's nose. The apparition stumbled back, and Roger flipped the table over to stand.

"No, he wasn't!" Roger stood over Christopher when Papa appeared in the doorway flanked by two other men.

"I assume you will come quietly, Mr. Mackie?" False culture and courtesy dripped from that voice.

Roger looked down at the man on the floor who was struggling to get back on his feet and said, "Yes, I want to see my kids."

"Very good. I'll take you to them." He waved the two men into the room and said," Do get Mr. Post up off the floor. He has some," there was a pause as Papa chose a word. "Things he needs to answer for." He turned to go. "Right this way, Mr. Mackie."

ALICE

Roger walked away, following Papa, to the sounds of those two men not lifting Mr. Post off the floor.

Dale had been awake a little while when Ethan was brought in, though she didn't move from where she curled in the corner. James was nowhere to be seen. Once the people, a man and a woman, Dale recognized the man, had left she went to check on Ethan. He was breathing. His pulse was steady. Good signs. She retreated back to the far end of the room and sat down.

"Okay, we've apparently been kidnapped by zombies. Except zombies can't kidnap people. They can't open doors. They can't think. They aren't zombies. So, what are they?"

Ethan didn't answer her question. Instead, he just looked at her with a blank stare which proceeded to travel around the room before a half-smile cracked his face.

"Another prison." Then he snorted and shook his head.

"Yeah." Dale smiled too. "Guess we have to stage another breakout."

"Just as soon as the rest of the team gets here, we can plan our great escape," Ethan said.

The two shared a chuckle and settled down to wait. A half hour later, Roger Mackie was escorted into the room and shut in. He looked at the two sitting on the floor and spread his hands helplessly.

"Looks like we've been captured again," Roger said.

Dale and Ethan burst out laughing.

"We just had that conversation. We were just waiting on you and James to show up so we could make an escape," said Dale.

"I thought James was with you," Roger said.

The laughter died somewhere between their heads and the ceiling, cut off abruptly by the realization or perhaps the memory that James had been lying next to Dale. Now Dale was in the cell, but James wasn't.

"I thought he was with one of you," Dale said.

" I left him in the bed with you. Ethan and I found your shoes earlier," Roger explained.

"In the bed with you," Ethan repeated. Dale smacked him on the shoulder.

"Not like that!" Dale paced, sticking her knuckles in her mouth. "Where do you think they've taken him?"

"I don't know, but I doubt we're going to have to wait long to find out."

The candles burned down. No one came to replace them, leaving the three sitting in shadow as the day and night wore on. It was late. They could feel it more than see it when someone finally came and opened the door. Two burly men walked in with a girl Ethan recognized.

"Charlotte?" Ethan glowered.

"I told you I would bring you to your friends. Now come quietly. It's time," she said.

"Time for what?" Ethan stood up and brushed his hands on his pants.

"Communion," Charlotte grinned.

The three shared a look before following Charlotte out of the room. The corridor they entered was tight, the walls too close to make running an option. Each of the men seemed to dominate it with their bodies, creating moving flesh walls to keep them going in the right direction. Charlotte's lantern made the only light. In silence, they walked until they reached a set of stairs. Up the stairs, there was more light and people moving around, a gathering.

When they ascended the stairs, they were in what could have been called a church. The pews the assembled sat on had certainly come from one, oak benches with bright blue cushions running the length. At one end of the room was a massive portrait covered with cloth. Above it, the sigil of the creature was painted on the wall. Everyone sat facing it. In front of the portrait, slumped in and tied to his wheelchair, was James. Dale reached for him and Roger pulled her back without a word. She settled back at his side.

Charlotte stopped in the center of the pews and held up her lantern. In response, a dozen other lanterns were raised and placed at the edges of the room throwing light toward the center. Only the space near the front remain dark. Until Papa entered with a lantern of his own, it threw not just light but symbols on the floor as well.

"Bring them forward, Charlotte, my love." His tone was softer, and he beckoned with one hand as one calling a child. She led the way forward, her lantern held high. There was no hiding the deformity in the faces now, or the blood which bathed certain parts of their body, or the stench Ethan had tried to ignore.

"My kin," Papa began. "We have been given safety and prosperity by the hand of our keeper." With one hand, he indicated the covered portrait. "And in return, we have bound ourselves to his will. Have we not?"

A murmured yes ran through the crowd, rising, cresting, and falling like an ocean wave of sound. The flames inside the lanterns moved with it, wavering the shadows.

"Yes, we have," Papa said.

As they drew closer, Ethan saw how the old man's eyes stared off in different directions, then swiveled to take him in making him feel like prey before some new kind of lizard.

"It was Charlotte who first heard his voice, remember? My dear Charlotte who brought his likeness into our midst." Papa gazed down at Charlotte.

She stopped and bowed her head at the mention of her name and the group waited with her.

"Through his likeness I have come to know his mind and his ways. I have begun to grope the way through the dark for all of us that we may continue to have peace. That we may continue to prosper. That we may continue whilst all the world around us goes up in the flames of oblivion which only his true coming may quench. So that we may continue. Is this not true?"

Again, yes rose and crested, breaking against the senses. Ethan fought the urge to sneeze, covering his mouth with his hand. Dale and Roger did the same.

James stirred, eyes slipping open as he adjusted himself in the chair.

"It is true. And so that his coming may be complete and we may prosper, he has asked us to do a terrible thing. A horrible thing. Until now, he has offered us safety in return for our peace. Let us not raise a hand against his children.

Paint the mark upon our doors that they may know us as his and not bring their death to us. This has been so. Yet these have come."

Papa swept his hand toward the group.

"They have come to us as we once were, as unbelievers, but they come in the presence of this one, a Marked One, one who must die. The faithful must kill him so that he cannot stop the Keeper's coming. Yet he has offered them amnesty, let them renounce the Marked, renounce their hunt, and they may yet be saved. Let them take communion with us and they are free, as we are free."

Upright now, James observed his surroundings and tested his bonds.

"Can he not be saved also?" A man pointed at James.

"No, he cannot. He is marked impure, as his companion is marked, and they cannot be saved. Only those who bear no mark may be saved through his offering of grace."

"Are you honestly using the word 'grace' in reference to a monster currently depopulating the known world?" Roger asked. Papa's face converted to a snarl as he turned to him, making him less lizard and more rat.

"He has kept us safe. He will keep you safe, if you will only give up your quest." Papa pulled away the curtain over the portrait, showing it to the room. "Give him your allegiance and you will be safe."

"Son," Christopher Post stood a few feet away, holding his hands out to his boy. "You can be safe here with me."

Ethan stared at his father's roaming eyes and disjointed features. A sick feeling slid through his stomach at the realization he could see his father in that face and hear him in that voice, but this couldn't possibly be his father. This monster made by a monster was just another zombie.

"You're not my Dad," Ethan said, turning to face the pulpit from which Papa spoke. "And we're not interested in your offer. Cut James loose."

"Does he speak for you all?" Papa asked.

"Yeah, I've found this kid turns out to occasionally be pretty bright. I'm with him." Roger's sentence was punctuated with a *thud*.

Then two more in rapid succession.

It came from the outside door. Two more and the doors split, falling like leaves to either side of the doorway and two Walkers shouldered their way into the building. Someone screamed. Someone else yelled. The Walkers ran forward as people scattered. Several of the pews were thrown aside with people were still on them. The snapping of wood covered the snapping of bone fairly well.

In the commotion, Dale made for James's wheelchair as the man tried to untie himself.

"We need to go," he said as she got close.

"Kinda got that," she said. Roger and Ethan were there with her moments later.

"Stop!"

Papa stood at his podium, now he held up his hands to the creatures running amok through his church. They both turned toward him as if noticing him for the first time, their breathing in sync as one.

"Take him. He is yours." He pointed to James and those gathered around him. "They are yours. We wish only your ascendance."

The two Walkers started at the group.

"Ethan, favor," James said.

"What?"

"Old man's lantern! Grab it. We need it," James said.

Ethan ducked the first swipe and hit the side of the podium hard enough to rock it. The lantern hit the floor with a cracking sound, but the fire stayed inside. The Walker, no longer interested in him, continued toward James who had now grabbed the wheels of his wheelchair and was pumping furiously for the other side of the room. They gave chase.

It was a form of stock car race none of them had ever seen before: a man in a wheelchair outpacing two grotesque monsters as he lapped the room. As he came back toward the podium, James shouted," Ethan, light up that portrait."

Cradling the lantern against his body like a football, Ethan lunged for the uncovered portrait and made the mistake of raising his eyes. From a distance, he hadn't been able to make out the details in the dark, but the creature portrayed before he offered no sense of benevolence. In fact, the name 'world eater' came to mind, a face made of teeth and tentacles, a body built to brush mountains, and eyes, those eyes able to suck out souls.

Papa hit him from the side, knocking him to the floor.

"You can't!" Papa shouted.

They wrestled for the lantern until Roger took Papa by the waist and spun him out onto the floor, right in front of James's wheelchair. They collided and James slid from the chair. One of the Walkers stepped on Papa, his body crushing flat and oozing under that foot. It left a bloody smear as it kept running to grab James with one massive hand and squeeze.

James flailed a moment, grabbed a hold of the monster's wrist and swung his hips as hard as he could. His useless feet *thudded* against the creature's chest and the second one grabbed them. He screamed in pain.

"Ethan! Get it moving!!"

Dale's scream brought Ethan back to the lantern in his hand, but the sound of something ripping got his attention. The Walker's wrist, the one holding James was coming apart as James pulled it in opposing directions. The creature roared with pain, its much smaller other arm trying to do something useful and finding nothing. James's face had contorted to the look commonly reserved for Alice. Ethan looked down, startled, as Dale snatched the lantern out of his hand.

"Dumbass," Dale snapped.

She took the lantern and smashed it at the base of the painting, smiling as the flames crawled their way up the paint and obliterated the face. It went faster than it should have, but she didn't care.

The Walkers caught fire and collapsed, dropping James to the floor where he lay on his back for a moment before turning over with an unnatural speed and began to crawl. He reached Papa and laid there, eye to eye with the old man.

"Don't feel terribly safe now. Do you?" James asked.

The flames reached the ceiling and started to vine their way across it.

"Time to go," Roger said as he righted the wheelchair.

"Our gear!" Dale pointed out.

"Leave it. We don't have time to look for it," Roger said.

Those who had survived were shuffling now, their bodies no longer their own. The lights in their eyes had gone out, leaving behind the nothing Ethan was all too familiar. He scanned the crowd of them milling about, knowing they would soon notice the living beings among them, smoke or no smoke, and tried to find his father. There he was, Christopher Post, his back against the wall. He was twitching as if he'd been shocked, his limps flapping ragdoll like. Ethan took a step toward him. It was James who pulled him back.

"No use. Leave him. I'm sorry," James said.

"I am too." Ethan sighed.

The school was still burning the next morning when they set out, gouts of smoke joining the thick gray clouds stretching from horizon to horizon.

"How did you know torching the painting would work?" Dale walked along beside James's wheelchair.

"I didn't." He nibbled on one ragged nail before starting to roll again.

"Then why'd you tell Ethan to do it?"

"Just thought it would. Didn't know it would, thought it would. Intuition." He popped a wheelie with the chair. "I'm just glad it did work. I didn't have a plan B."

"You dumbass." Dale laughed.

"Still adore me, right?"

"Yeah, I guess I do." She squeezed his shoulder.

The group had gone three miles from the town, a road marker telling them they could strike out west or continue going north and east. Roger stopped. He looked at both roads. There was no mistaking the sky being darker further east. The other three looked at him.

"You don't have to go with me," James said pointing his chair to the East. "I understand if you don't want to. I can make it there on my own now that I know where I'm going."

"By yourself?" Roger asked.

"Yes, by myself." He turned his back to them and crossed his arms over his chest. Dale put her hand on the wheelchair handle.

"Not by yourself," Dale said.

Ethan shook his head and rubbed a hand through his hair, it was getting thicker and shaggier. His eyes trailed West, then East.

"It took your Dad," Dale said.

"No. My Dad gave up," Ethan said. "He wanted safety and..." Ethan turned west. "He got it."

"Still..." Dale continued.

Ethan turned his head sharply at Dale's word.

"Still what? That thing played on his fear, now you think I'm giving in to mine?" Ethan asked her.

"I don't think I'm going with you." Roger's unsteady declaration brought them all to a halt.

"What?" Ethan turned to Roger.

"Obsession and adventure are for young people. At my age..." Roger said, shaking his head.

"At your age you should be dandling a grandkid on your knee, not trying to slay dragons. Or whatever the hell that thing is." James sighed. "Come or don't come, Roger, no one is going to hold it against you."

Ethan let his eyes slide from Roger to the ground. Roger who wasn't going any further, he was giving up the fight. Dale wasn't, but Dale and James were...together of sorts. He didn't know what they were, but friends seemed to be the least of it. And Alice, with Alice gone did they really have a chance?

"And what happens even if we do manage to stop this thing? What will change?" Ethan asked them.

"I don't know," James said with a shrug. "But I would rather find out than live with not knowing."

"We've got to see this through," Ethan said, lifting his head. He nodded 'yes' and started walking down the road toward Senora. "Roger, *we* have got to see this through."

The older man shook his head then caught up with them.

"Then let's see this through," Roger said.

In the far East over the ocean, the sky was gunmetal gray and smoke black the color of heavy storms, the promise of all hell coming to earth.

CHAPTER EIGHTEEN

The Lighthouse

THEY PROBABLY WOULDN'T HAVE STOPPED at the faux Victorian house except night had fallen, making the already dark sky even darker, and there were cars parked in every direction on the road ahead. A tattered banner hung across the front porch area declaring "WELCOME TO SENORA, the QUAINTEST LITTLE TOWN BY THE SEA".

"Why does that give me the feeling like there is a Disney World in Hell?" James said.

"What makes you think there isn't?" Dale leaned over the handles of James's wheelchair and ruffled his hair.

"Mind the do, chipmunk."

He eyed the stairs.

"You maneuver the chair. I'll get me." James climbed down with the ease of practice and scooted his way over to the stairs climbing all four fairly quickly as Dale levered the wheelchair up each one.

"Missed the Disabilities Act from the looks of things. This place isn't disabled accessible."

Roger tromped up the stairs and opened the door to the house which lead into what had once been a living room/ dining room combo.

"Yeah, well, can't blame a monster from the bottom of the ocean for not realizing everyone isn't going to have working legs," Roger said.

"That monster didn't build this." Ethan's statement got a look of exasperation from James who was climbing back into his chair and maneuvering it into the building itself.

Dale rolled her eyes. "Sorry."

"It's okay," Dale said. "We're all tired."

Day had ceased to truly mean much with the constant gray haze of clouds blocking out the sun. They traveled for as long as the sky held light and when darkness fell, either because another storm rolled in or night truly fell, they found a sort of safe place and bedded down until the dark departed. Progress was sporadic, but they were finally in Senora. For whatever good that would do them.

Inside was a kiosk with a map of the town. There wasn't much to it. A main street running all the way to the marina. A town square full of quaintly decorated old buildings meant to mimic what the place had been when settlers first found themselves there. A lighthouse set on a crag looking down on the city from a bluff partly crumbling into the ocean, if the map's indication of it being on an island was correct. James poured over the map with it inches from his face as the others moved around, searching the place.

"There isn't any blood," Dale said as she made her way back into the living room area and dropped onto a long bench with six purple cushions and one red one in the center.

"There hasn't been any in the last three places we've stopped," James said, looking up from the map. "And we haven't seen a Walker since Bruston."

Bruston had been the last time they'd fired a gun, just as well since they had lost nearly everything with the fire.

Now they each only had a small pistol, not much against a Walker. Better to run from them than get into an unwinnable fire fight. Instead, they shattered a window with a bullet and then disappeared when the creature went rushing toward the sound.

"That's strange." Roger rejoined them and began to leaf through brochures for excursions over by what might have once been an information desk. He snatched one up with a cry. "James, come look at this."

"Easier if you bring it over here. This thing doesn't like carpet."

Roger shoved the brochure under James's nose.

"Look familiar?" Roger asked.

Dale and Ethan, who had come in from his time up the stairs, peered over his shoulder. The man in the photograph looked like James, but he wasn't James. For one, he had no tattoos. For two, both of his eyes were one color: green. Yet the family resemblance was there.

"Summers's Charter Fishing Expeditions," James read the title. "Summers. Matthew Summers." His eyes roamed the picture as he said the name.

"Do you know him?" Ethan asked.

"I..." James stumbled over the word and took the brochure in his hands. "I." He closed his eyes. "I, think, I do." He turned the glossy paper over before opening it. Inside were more pictures of the same man, sometimes beside large fish. In one, he stood next to a beautiful boat, The *Victoria Alice* according to the name painted on the side. "I've been on that boat." His tone was certain even as his hands began to shake. With a spasm, he crushed the paper in his hands. "Matthew's boat. My bike. Victoria. Alice." His whole body shuddered.

ALICE

Dale pressed her face to the side of his neck and wrapped her arms around James's shoulders.

When he dropped the brochure, it was Ethan who picked it up and smoothed the paper. The final photo was of Matthew standing at the lighthouse.

"Say's the Charters pick up at his home near the old Senora Sound Lighthouse across the land bridge on Keeper's Island."

Ethan turned to Roger who nodded.

"Once the weather clears, for now, we're stuck here," Roger said.

The lightning snapped outside followed by a roll of thunder punctuated his sentence with an exclamation point. Rain began to drum against the windows.

"Beautiful music to sleep to," Ethan said.

Midnight rolled in with the thunder still walking from horizon to horizon and rain lashing the house. James opened his eyes and turned over on his side. Dale was already up looking out the window.

"Your friend is back," she said. "We haven't seen her in a while either."

"I thought I felt her." James levered himself up enough to scoot over to her and take a hold of her legs. "Is she saying anything?"

"I can only just make her out from here." Placing a hand on his hair, she knelt to his level. "I'm going to go out there."

"Roger will yell at you."

"Not if you don't tell him." She smiled. "And why would you do that?"

"Dale." He wrapped his arms around her then, hugging her hard. "Come back."

"I plan on it." She kissed his temple and waited for him to let go. It took him a few seconds, but he did, and she headed to the front door on quiet feet. Dale slipped out into the rain and the door clicked shut behind her.

Outside, she shielded her eyes with her hand, the heavy droplets striking and soaking her to the skin, but there she was standing in the rain, a little girl in a blue school jumper with a white shirt growing a bright red blossom of blood on her chest. Dale ran to her and the girl turned to her, wide eyes brown and green. She smiled; a child's smile full of happiness. So close, Dale couldn't help noticing the gold necklace with a wire name "Alice" at her throat. It was a surprise when the girl threw herself forward and wrapped her arms around Dale's neck.

"Thank you."

The words came to Dale's ears like they were yelled up from the bottom of the well.

"Who are you?" Dale asked.

"She'll need him," the little girl said. "He needs him."

"Who?"

The little girl ignored the question stepping back and pointing to the horizon. "Go."

Above the town, the lighthouse flickered to life, a bright blue spotlight turning the falling rain in a million prisms. A howl of suffering competed with the storm for sound as the light swept the buildings. Dale turned back to where the little girl had stood to find her gone. She wiped her eyes hard as if it would bring the girl back. Running back to the porch, Dale let herself feel how her heart was hammering in her chest, beating harder than the earth hurled rain.

Roger was, predictably, waiting for her when she was reentered. James sat on the floor not far from the door, his eyes glazed and empty. Ethan knelt by James, checking his pulse.

"What the hell happened? James screamed and you were gone," Roger said.

"The lighthouse is on," Dale answered.

"What?"

Ethan peered out the window.

"The little girl came back. I went to see because James couldn't." Dale dropped down next to James and shook him. "We're going to the lighthouse. I think Alice might be there."

Alice had to be the 'She', but who was the 'He'?

"Alice?" Ethan asked, coming back. "What makes you think that?"

"The girl said 'She would need him' talking about James." She shook James hard. "Wake up."

He came back, eyes rolling into focus. His face slid into an expression of misery.

"Matthew. She was supposed to bring us back to you," James mumbled.

"She who, James?" Dale asked.

He didn't answer, shaking his head and biting his lip.

"James, what's at the lighthouse?" Ethan asked.

He didn't answer that either. A sob quaked his chest.

"I think we need to go to the lighthouse now," Ethan said. "Screw the rain."

"According to that brochure, the only way out to that jut of rock is a land bridge. With the weather this bad, there's no way it's not covered. We're going to have to wait this out," Roger said.

"What if we can't?" Dale pulled her fingers through James's hair since he wasn't in the mood to notice. "Wait, I mean. What if we're needed there now?"

Above the storm sounds, that howl came again, vocal despair. James echoed it. As he continued without breathing, they stopped frozen. Done, he hung his head and panted.

"He can't keep the light on," James gasped. "And she's not strong enough alone." Falling over, he crawled for the door.

"James, wait." Roger took a hold of the back of James's shirt and slid as the man kept going. "Wait!"

Without explanation, James kept moving, elbows and hands digging into the floor as he lurched along. Roger leaned back and bodily pulled James up off the floor and Ethan helped him to get the man upright and then into his wheelchair.

"I guess we're going," Ethan said.

Once James was in his chair, he was rolling for the door, the others following him out into the driving rain.

Main Street was, unremarkably empty, a stretch of blacktop through the center of a small town. James rolled down it quiet, his eyes forward and arms pumping the wheels as fast as he could. The others jogged to keep up. The Town Square opened up on either side of Main Street and James slowed, head going up like a dog scenting something on the wind.

"Get back!" he ordered.

The storm ate his words, but his sudden stop brought the others to a halt as well, so when the creature barreled past in front of him, they weren't in the way. It skidded on the wet in the dark and turned toward them. It wasn't a Walker. Humanity had never created anything remotely like this. The face alone gave it kinship to mortals. The body was something else, a mish mash of things belonging more to the water than land. Dale swallowed hard as it leveled its gaze at them, *thudding* toward them more slowly now.

James backed up as it came forward, giving ground.

ALICE

It whipped around suddenly, and the group could only watch as it was hit with something. Something that knocked it down and then levered it hard into the side of a building. As it rose again, Alice rolled her shoulders, her jaw was broken and hung by tatters of skin and muscle, but there was no mistaking the pleasure in her face.

It screamed. She screamed back. They met in the middle of the street with a sound of something shattering. The thing didn't get back up as Alice stood over it. The head turned to look up at her and she ground a heel directly into one of its eyes. It stopped moving.

Ethan was halfway to Alice before she turned to face them. Her eyes sparkled red against the gray rain. Dale swung Ethan out of the way as Alice grabbed for him. Then James was again between them and her.

"Alice!" he shouted.

The monster in Alice looked at the four of them as if they were nothing more than the animal she had just put down.

"Alice!" James screamed her name again as she took him by the front of his shirt and held him up dangling from her fists. "No." He sputtered. "Not Alice." Choking, he found the breath to call her name. "Victoria!"

Alice reeled back and dropped him. He missed the chair by inches, knocking his head against the arm before he hit the ground.

"Victoria." He reached for her; his hand opened as if he would cast a spell on her. "Victoria. Sister. Wife. Mother. Victoria." He yelled the words over the rolling thunder. "Victoria. Sister of James. Wife of Matthew. Mother of Alice! Fight him!"

Her long fingers peeled back her dreads, exposing her face and painfully bright red eyes.

"Remember me," he whispered. "Please remember me, Victoria."

The air split with lightning leaving behind the scent of ozone followed by a rumble of thunder Alice knelt in the rain, unmoving. James began to crawl toward her, but Ethan pulled him back. As the rain pelted down on them all, Alice was a statue. Then she raised her head. Her eyes were predatory.

"Run." James screamed and began to pump his arms to make the chair lurch forward. On the rain slick streets, it left a fan of spray. The others did their best to keep up. Alice hadn't moved. Instead, she watched them go. Her lips trembled as she counted time.

100 seconds. She gave them one hundred seconds. Then she rolled her to feet and started after them at a flat run.

Waves crashed against the land bridge as Roger came to a panting stop.

"Come on!" Ethan shouted.

"I can't keep running," Roger said, holding his side.

James and Dale got ahead as Ethan stopped to give Roger his arm. Roger shook him off.

"Go. I'll slow her down," Roger said.

"You're not even a speed bump to her," Ethan countered. "Come on."

"Maybe not, but you'd better go before I find out."

Ethan jogged a few steps, then turned back. Roger stood in the rain at the end of the bridge with his back to him. Throwing himself forward, Ethan clasped the old man hard.

"Don't die." Ethan felt tears well in his eyes.

"Go, kid." Roger patted his arms and shivered when the younger man let him go. Ethan ran for it without looking back again, trying to catch up with James and Dale.

ALICE

The rock the lighthouse stood on loomed up out of the dark like a sudden predator before the lightning could define its shape. The sides were almost sheer from long years but cut into the sides were steps. James stopped at the bottom and looked up those steps.

"No way. We don't have the time," James said.

"Hurry up," said Dale.

"You'll have to go without me."

"Didn't I already say I wasn't leaving you?" James and Dale's voices had risen to screams against the weather.

James shook his head.

"Go. Just keep going. The answers are up there." He pointed up the stairs and snapped his head around at the ghost of a scream on the wind.

"Roger." Ethan joined them just in time to give it a name. "What are we waiting on?"

"Dale to leave me," James said. "Take her and head for the top."

"What about you?" Ethan asked.

"I can't make it. Too slow. Maybe she'll trip over me."

Ethan grabbed Dale by the waist.

"Let's go, short stuff," Ethan said.

"Where's Roger?" Dale asked.

"He stayed behind. Get moving," Ethan said.

Ethan was glad he couldn't see Dale's face as he started taking the stairs as fast as he could, dragging her along.

James slipped out of his chair and onto the cold ground. The rain made pinging noises off the metal. Another ghost of a scream drifted to his ears over the racket. Swallowing hard, he curled up as small as he was able. Maybe she'd miss him in the dark, his sister-in-law.

Or maybe she'd kill him quick.

Either or.

The light high above made the small clearing where the lighthouse itself sat practically noontime even in the heavy dark. The beam illuminated the nearby sea, choppy and rough, with the nasty weather. The pair made it to the door and took shelter under the eaves.

"Look!" Dale pointed to what might have been an attempt at a house addition. The wood had already started to show signs of damage, but it was the beginning of a wheelchair ramp. One that would allow access into the lighthouse itself.

"Preparations?" Ethan asked.

"I don't know."

The door gave after Ethan put his shoulder to it a few times, splintering inward with a crash. The house smelled faintly of vanilla even under the wet smell from an open window letting in the elements. Ethan took in a deep breath and was surprised to find Dale doing the same.

"Smells like home," she said.

"Yeah."

The foyer led in three directions, a living room, a kitchen, and a set of stairs. They turned into the living room and looked around. It was a common space with a ratty couch, a television set, and all the comfortable knick-knacks associated with family living. On a bookcase across from the television, there were photographs along with the books. Some of the books were children's books done in bright colors easily read in the pouring light. A wedding photo presided over the room. Ethan reached up to take it down.

"Matthew and Victoria," he read. He recognized the man in the photo from the brochure and the woman he was standing beside with a giant smile was a woman he had slept beside. Victoria was smiling in the photograph looking directly at the camera. Behind them both, James stood looking over the man's shoulder a grin of his own plastered to his face as he gave the man bunny ears.

"James called her Victoria," Dale said. "He said Alice was her daughter, not her."

Nearby, something *thudded* and the ever-present light faltered.

"James said there would be answers here. We should find them before Alice or whoever she is finds us."

"Split up?" Ethan asked.

"That's how people die in horror movies, you know," Dale said.

"Yeah, but if we don't hurry, we may die anyway. So, let's move."

Ethan crossed the foyer into the kitchen and Dale inched her way up the stairs. The scent of vanilla was stronger up the stairs. There had been no wind to dissipate it. The stairs wound up, past a landing, and then further up into the dark. The door on the landing had a name written across the front in large sparkly letters, "ALICE". The door squeaked as Dale pushed on it.

Inside was a little girl's room done in pale blues and greens to mimic under the sea. On the wall, a mermaid had been painted sitting on a seashell and doing her hair in a mirror. The mirror the mermaid was using was an actual mirror, reflecting nothing at all. Dale crossed toward it and waved her hand in front of it, yet it remained dark. Until the next flash of lightning when a face, the same little girl Dale had seen earlier appeared in it.

Her hands were pressed against the inside of the mirror and she stared out at Dale with wide eyes. Her mouth moved slowly.

"I love you, Momma." Dale repeated before she turned around. Victoria's first swing went over her head, leaving Dale an opening to make for the door.

"Ethan!" She nearly collided with him on the staircase as she came tumbling out of the room with the woman in tow.

"Run!" They both headed up the stairs with her only a step or so behind.

They burst onto the platform with the lighthouse light and shielded their eyes before throwing themselves to the floor. Rolling over they were just in time to see Alice's silhouette as she came across the floor toward them. With one hand, she snatched Dale up by her collar and dangled her with her toes a foot off the ground.

"Alice, no," Ethan said as he scrambled to his feet. The light turned again, forcing him to cover his eyes. When he opened them again, the room had changed. They were no longer in a lighthouse lashed by an unnatural storm, but at a breakfast table. A man and a woman sat at the table with a little girl.

"What?"

Dale stood across the room, her arms hugged around herself.

CHAPTER NINETEEN

How It All Began

MATTHEW SPOONED IN A MOUTHFUL OF runny eggs and smiled. Victoria smiled back over the head of their little girl. The room smelled of fried bacon and eggs with an undertone of vanilla. A simple homey kitchen where a family undoubtedly took a number of meals, just like they were on that particular morning.

"I don't get how you can make me smile on my worst day," Matthew said.

Even as he spoke, the smile was dying on his lips.

"That's why you married me." Victoria got up from her seat and kissed him on the forehead before doing the same to the little girl. "Eat up. You've got to get to school."

Ethan recognized her from James's description. She was the lost girl. The one they'd been following.

"Mom, are you leaving?" young Alice asked.

The two adults looked almost shocked and then Victoria knelt down next to the chair and pulled her long hair out of her face.

"Do you remember when we went to see your Uncle James? And you got to play in his wheelchair while they gave him a sponge bath?"

"Yeah."

"Well, your Daddy and I have decided Uncle James doesn't need to be so far away. He needs to be closer so we can take care of him and you can spend time with him. So, Mommy is going out to get him ready to come live with us."

"That's why you cleaned out the empty room?"

"Yes. It's going to be your Uncle James's room. But that means Mommy is going to go away for a while, okay?"

"It also means Dad and Alice get to go out on a special trip. Won't that be fun?" Matthew said.

"Mom, are you scared?" Alice asked.

Victoria grimaced and shook her head yes.

"A little bit, pumpkin. I don't like to fly, and I've got to go all by myself."

"Why can't Daddy and I go with you?"

"Because Daddy's got a charter and you've got school. So, you need to finish your breakfast."

Alice looked from one to the other slowly. Ethan thought for a moment she paused on him. Then she said," Mom shouldn't have to go by herself." The little girl pulled the necklace off her neck, a bent wire version of her name and hung it around her mother's neck solemnly. "Now I can go with you and protect you from the fear."

"Thank you, baby. Finish your eggs."

"But Mom, I don't want eggs."

"Eat your eggs, Alice Anne. You ate the bacon."

The room turned light again, dissolving into brightness. Ethan threw his arm over his eyes.

The light in the lighthouse turned, leaving Dale in shadow, where she hung from Victoria's hands. They were both statue-still. Ethan stumbled toward them.

"The necklace."

It wasn't around Victoria's neck anymore. Where was it? She had given it to Dale before she disappeared. Ethan remembered Dale showing it to him in wonder after she was gone.

"Please, don't have lost it," he mumbled to himself

He searched Dale's pockets as the light swung around again.

It stole the room, replacing it with what he was certain was a boat. Matthew sat on a runner board next to another man, both of them wearing scuba gear.

"Double check your hoses to be sure everything is working. We don't want to get down there and end up with problems."

"Of course." His charter appeared less interested in checking his equipment and more on getting into the water. The two splashed in and disappeared beneath the waves.

Unbidden, Ethan went with them. Down until it seemed they would find the bottom and then even deeper. They entered cleft in the rock to excited gesturing from the man. They surfaced inside a cave.

"I didn't believe it was here." The man climbed out of the water slowly, encumbered by his equipment. "It wasn't supposed to be true."

He tried to run with the tank attached but ended up falling forward then crawling toward what Ethan thought looked like something out of an ancient Greek myth on acid. Those were columns, but they wandered on their way to the ceiling, white and dirty brown by turns as if the marble had gone piebald. Matthew was too far behind to stop him from disappearing into the darkness.

"Come back here." Matthew's shoulders slumped. "Damnit. I'm responsible for his stupid ass." He started into the dark after him, shedding the oxygen tank as he went. He wasn't too excited to think about maneuverability. Ethan followed the two men into the dark.

The sense of being in a Greek temple continued down the hallway lined with human shaped busts with alien faces, their features resembling creatures. The piebald marble made their footsteps echo with a startling sharpness. The corridor, sheathed in it, continued forward for a time before opening into a great chamber.

"The *One from the Trench* wasn't supposed to be real." The scholar's voice had reached the pitch of childish, gleeful babbling.

Matthew looked decidedly less impressed.

They stood in the center of a vast cavern lit by some light source Ethan couldn't make out. Up ahead, an altar made of some light color stone, maybe limestone, streaked with old blood. The scholar was leaning across it trying to reach something on the far side.

"I've been gathering references to him for fifteen years, but everyone concluded he was nothing more than a myth. Just something the ancients made up." The stream of words continued unabated as he grasped the statuette on the far side with pale hands. "But here it is, proof. A temple. A carving. Real Proof."

The man turned and as he did his voice lowered into menacing." And I'll be the one who brings it into the light."

The wall exploded with white light and Ethan found himself scrambling to search through Dale's pockets before the next wave. The light swung slowly toward him again.

"Dale, where did you put it?" he cursed.

Then he noticed the glint at her neck. Dale was *wearing* Alice's necklace.

Ethan found himself back in the same temple, but this time it was young Alice standing there with her father. He saw the body of the scholar laid beside the altar. His body was contorted with agony and his face a mask of fear and pain. Matthew carried Alice to the altar and set her down on it.

"Daddy," she said. "Daddy, what's happening? This place is scary."

"It's okay, Pumpkin. It's going to be fine. We're going to be making a brand-new world. A world where everyone will be happy."

The statuette stood over the altar looking down it with avid eyes. Alice looked up into the face of the statue and squeezed her eyes shut.

"Daddy, I wanna go home!!"

Matthew brought his hand up and it flashed down. The blade bit into Alice's chest and sprayed blood. Her multi-colored eyes flew wide as she screamed, "Mommy!"

The world exploded.

Ethan snatched the necklace from around Dale's neck, feeling the clasp give under the pressure. The light faded now, going out even as it went around. Victoria's eyes moved, her fingers tightened, even as Dale wriggled in her grip. He had to lean up to get the necklace around Victoria's neck and tried to close it. The clasp was broken.

"Shit. Shit. Shit," he cursed as he tried to close it. "Please. Please. Please work."

A tiny hand pressed the clasp closed and the chain hung gold against Victoria's brown skin. She dropped Dale to the floor of the lighthouse as the light finally guttered and went out.

I love you, Mommy.

Ethan heard the whisper as Victoria shook her head, clearing her eyes.

"Ethan. Dale." Victoria sounded dazed.

"Victoria?"

"Yes."

"Where are Roger and James?"

"I don't know."

Panic flashed across her features and she ran for the stairs. Ethan was only steps behind, and Dale followed.

The world beyond the lighthouse remained a mess of rain and flying surf as she took the stairs down, sliding into the walls in places. Ethan shielded his eyes and made his way down slower, uncertain, along with Dale. At the bottom, the wheelchair knocked against the wall whenever it was hit by a wave.

"James!" Victoria screamed.

The thrashing world swallowed her voice, but she shouted his name again. No response. The others found her clutching the arms of the metal chair and screaming her brother-in-law's name over and over again, as if that would bring him back. Ethan grabbed her by her upper arm.

"We need to go back."

A wave pushed him hard against the cliff wall and Dale had to huddle as small as she could to keep from being swept off the side. Her look almost made him let go, but he held her gaze and her arm.

"We have to go."

Roger would have wanted them to survive. Would have done everything he could to make sure they did. If he gave his life, better not to waste theirs. Another wave towered high and crashed into the land bridge, engulfing it in sea water. They needed to be on the high ground. Sputtering,

Ethan jerked on Victoria's arm and headed for the stairs. Dale grabbed hold of his shirt as he passed, using him as a shield against some of the weather's rage.

Inside of the lighthouse home, they collapsed. The open door let in the wind and rain. The waves became a distant sound, not forgotten, but no longer a threat. Victoria clasped her knees to her chest and stared out the open door.

She repeated three names under her breath as a mantra.

Alice. James. Matthew.

CHAPTER TWENTY

Let's Take Him the Fight

DALE WOKE UP WITH ETHAN CURLED CLOSE and froze. For a moment, she thought it was James, but the memory of his loss was still too fresh to fade. She crawled out from under Ethan's arm. Victoria sat in the middle of the hallway floor. What passed for daylight streamed in through the open door. Victoria looked haggard, her face drawn and tired. Dale put her hand on her shoulder.

"You didn't sleep."

"No." Victoria was quiet, almost the tone one would use at a funeral. "I was waiting. Hoping..." The word trailed off into nothing.

They sat in silence until Ethan rolled over and declared," Are we in hell?"

"Not yet," Dale said. "But I'm pretty sure the thing responsible is going to try and put us there."

"It doesn't want to kill humanity. Just rule it. Alice tried to save us," Victoria said.

"What?" Ethan asked.

"She kept trying to stop it, but things aren't going well. She's losing. It's too big. Too old. Too powerful. James and I were all she had left to cling to after he..."

Victoria shoved up off the floor, breaking Dale's grip on her shoulder.

"After she died."

"After he killed her," Ethan said. He sat on the floor, looking up at her, his head thrown back. "Your husband killed your daughter and unleashed that thing."

She looked away.

"So, what do we do now?" Dale asked.

"We keep going. We know where it is, sorta. We take the fight to it. Find a way to destroy it. Someway to stop what's happening." Victoria's weary voice still held a spark of hope.

"What if there isn't a way?" asked Dale.

"Do you have something to go home to?" Ethan asked.

Dale paled at the question and the look in Ethan's eyes. He was right though. None of them had anything left. "Can you get us to where that thing is hiding?"

"Yes." Victoria straightened, her chin coming up and shoulders squaring back.

Dale made herself stand and find that same confident stance, even if her knees didn't feel it. "And if the spare gear is still at the marina, the dive won't be a problem."

"Then let's go collect what it owes," Ethan said.

The only way to the marina was back across the land bridge and into the harbor proper. They traveled on foot through a day the color of twilight until Ethan held up a hand.

"You hear that?" Ethan leaned into hear better.

They strained to hear. Victoria turned and started back toward the lighthouse island. The coughing grew louder as they got closer.

"Who's there?" Ethan called.

A pale hand shot out from a hole in the rock. The owner took a deep breath.

"James?" Victoria called.

Another loud, slow, deep breath. It rattled its way down into the owner's lungs. Victoria took a hold of the arm and pulled. A loud exclamation and string of curses followed. There was no mistaking that voice.

"James!" She turned to the others.

Ethan helped pull while Dale looked on. James's head and shoulders popped out of the hole he'd shoved himself into.

"I'm stuck," he cried when his body refused to come further. They let go and reconsidered the situation.

"If we keep pulling, we're probably going to pull his skin off." Victoria crossed her arms over her chest while they thought about it.

"If we don't keep pulling, he's going to stay stuck there and starve," Ethan said.

"I'm hungry now though," James said.

Dale snickered.

"Figure out how to get yourself out of that hole and I've got an apple you can have." Dale produced a shiny, if a little beaten up, apple from her bag. It had come off the tree the day they entered the town. James locked eyes on it and followed it the way a dog would a treat.

"Promise?" James said.

"Pinkie swear." She offered him her free hand.

They shook on it. Ethan and Victoria slipped back as James put his hands on either side of the hole and pushed himself forward, turning his hips back and forth to free them from whatever it was that held him back. When he popped out of the hole, it was a scrapping sound and bit of blood, but Victoria caught him before he face-planted onto the rocks below his hiding place. She held him like a teddy bear, squeezing him tight.

"I thought you were dead," Victoria said.

"You're going to make me dead if you keep squeezing. Lay off, sis." He put his hands on her shoulders and pushed back.

"Sorry." Victoria smiled.

"Don't be. Where's my apple?" James said.

Dale gave him the promised apple and he chomped it down to the core in a few large bites.

"Great. Where's the rest of the food?"

"We'll eat later. Right now, we've got to save the world." Ethan almost sounded bright. Dale hugged him. They set off for the marina.

Roger didn't reappear out of the heavy mist hanging over the mainland as they made their way to the Senora marina. Matthew moored the *Victoria Alice* there. The boat wasn't in its dock, but floating, knocking against one of the docks as it waited for the outgoing tide to drag it back out. It looked as though it had barely survived the weather. Victoria and Ethan swam out to see if it could be docked properly to get everyone on board. Dale and James stayed on the dry land and waited.

"This place has been eerie quiet. We only saw that one Walker Victoria killed but nothing else. Where is everything else?" Dale asked.

"Why should there be anything else?" James asked.

"This close to the end is where all the big stuff happens in books."

"This isn't a book, Chipmunk. It's real life." James looked out over the water and rubbed his hands together. "When this is over..."

"Hm?"

"I was just wondering, when this is over..." He rubbed his hands more as though he were cold and smoothed his filthy pants.

"Waiting."

"Trying to figure out what to say. Gimme a minute. I'm no good at this sort of thing."

The wind ruffled his shaggy hair and he kept his gaze out over the ocean. Dale slid a little closer and laid her head against his shoulder.

"You know. I'd spend forever with you," she said. "If that's what you're asking." He stiffened and relaxed, putting his head against hers.

"Yeah, that's what I'm asking," James said.

"Then yeah. You and me. Forever."

"We make an awesome duo. The cripple and the chipmunk." Dale half-heartedly swatted him in the stomach.

"What? It's true."

"I am not a chipmunk."

"Nope, not a chipmunk." He grinned. "*My* chipmunk."

Victoria piloted the *Victoria Alice* into a docking space and Ethan hopped off, clad in no more than a pair of shorts.

"Let's go, you two."

He piggy-backed James up to the ladder and let him climb aboard to Victoria who picked him up.

"It's nice having you back when you aren't trying to kill me," James said.

"James, shut up." Victoria didn't sound all that upset.

"Taking over Roger's place?" James asked with a smirk.

The world went deaf as Victoria dropped him on the deck. James didn't even say 'ow'. He just looked up at her retreating back.

"Too soon," he said as he turned over and started to crawl. He moved across the deck slowly as Victoria piloted the boat out of dock and onto the open sea.

The land had disappeared in all directions when they stopped, leaving them with nothing but open water.

"Are you sure this is where we're supposed to be?" Ethan stared over the edge of the boat into the deep dark water.

"Yes." Victoria could feel the pull of the place.

"Then we had better suit up and get going," Ethan said.

Once they had pulled on the scuba gear, they dropped down into the cold water. The sea wasn't rough below the surface. It was a serene gray, growing a darker blue as they slid deeper. Victoria wore only a face mask, but she seemed to have no problem with either the lack of oxygen or the growing pressure as she led the way down. Matthew's notes, found onboard the ship, were enough to allow them to find the opening to the cave hidden in the chasm under the sea.

When they surfaced in the pool where he had once been, they were stunned to find it surrounded by marble. As if the temple had grown out to meet it. Climbing from the pool, they looked around. Dale was still unstopping her ears when Victoria motioned for quiet.

Chanting came from further in. It drifted back to them, washing over them then disappearing into the stillness of the pool.

They inched across the space, all too aware of how the sparse light thrown from the walls illuminated them. Dale did her best not to think about how much of an advantage the light gave those who were waiting on them. Out of the pool room there was a narrow, short corridor. It ended in a much larger room dominated on one end by the statue equivalent of the painting James had set fire to once upon a time.

"He doesn't get any prettier," Ethan said covering his mouth with his hand.

"No, he doesn't," Victoria said.

The room wasn't a church, though there was a deity and an altar at one end. There was no place to sit. Instead, a multitude knelt on the floor, chanting in low ominous tones, suggesting times when human sacrifice was the order of the day. Dale looked over the heads as best she could and suppressed a shudder at the realization there was fresh blood on the altar.

They drew back into the corridor.

"What do we do?" she asked.

"It knows we're here," Victoria said. "But it isn't doing anything. Like it's waiting on something."

The world shook as something made impact. It came from the pool room. Ethan saw it first.

"Oh God," he said, but his words were swallowed by the sound of running feet.

The cultists swarmed into the corridor and continued on in a mad rush. On the floor, James covered his head with his hands and remained still. The others flattened themselves out of the way. Ethan saw those who had been chanting throw themselves into the waiting arms of what he could only think of as a sea monster.

It snapped off heads with its beak and crammed bodies into its maw, stuffing itself like a starving man at a buffet. The tide of bodies slowed to a trickle, then petered off. Those who weren't taken in the immediate frenzy, waited their turn, swaying and moaning, until it swept them up in a symphony of broken bones and devoured them.

Dale looked down when a hand took hers and tugged hard.

"Come on," the little girl whispered. "He's distracted."

Grabbing a hold of Victoria, Dale eased back into the room with the statue. James followed, crawling along the floor, and Ethan, finally tearing his eyes away, brought up the rear. They were alone in the room with the statue, the final expression of some dark inhuman purpose. The room smelled of sweat, fear, and death. Left behind, possibly trampled in the fit of ecstasy, several bodies lay abandoned. Their faces cold-cast expressions of rapture. Dale concentrated on the altar.

"Have you come?" Those words whispered and floated toward them as a man stepped out from the shadows beside the altar. "Have you come?"

Matthew Summers stared at the group with eyes lit by passion as he drew a knife from behind his back.

"Come to feed the Master." He grinned at them.

He bounded across the space and Victoria caught him, holding him off.

"Do something," she said as the pair spun, and Matthew tried again to stab her in the chest with his weapon.

In the pool room, the creature roared. Ethan only missed having his legs taken off by a tentacle reaching down the corridor.

"Oh shit." The expletive leapt out of Dale's mouth as the battle between Victoria and Matthew knocked her to the floor. At one end of the room, two people, former lovers, fought like animals. At the other end, Ethan fended off the sea monster's probing arms. In between, Dale gathered herself back to her feet and looked at James.

"What do we do?" she asked.

"I don't know. Think of something," James replied.

"You only get uglier up close," she muttered as she climbed the altar. Standing on the surface, she could see where the blood had dripped down the sides from an indention in the center. The statuette stared at her with pupil-less eyes.

"Do something faster," yelled Ethan as he narrowly avoided another swipe. "This thing is still hungry."

"Dale, I've got an idea. Gimme the statue," James said.

It was small enough for James to carry as he crawled across the floor and right into the waiting tentacles of the creature. With a pained sound, he disappeared down the corridor and into the pool, where the creature waited.

"No!" Matthew tried to go after him, but Victoria wouldn't allow it. As he tried to disengage from Victoria, Matthew found himself thrown to the floor, his knife spinning away from his hand.

Without a moment's hesitation, the creature ate James and the statuette. Matthew went limp beneath Victoria and Victoria, herself, swayed. Dale watched as the little girl, Alice, flickered then appeared to her parents before taking hold of them both and disappearing. Their bodies remained. Their eyes were empty.

Beneath the waves, the creature struggled, then gasped its own final breath, before settling in the deep.

Ethan and Dale stared at the devastation.

"Did we win?" Ethan asked.

"I think so," Dale said.

There was no conviction in it.

None at all.

CHAPTER TWENTY-ONE

Ten Days Later

DALE LOOKED OUT THE WINDOW AND OVER the water to the horizon. It grew dark with thunder clouds again. Another storm. Another night they waited it out. Since returning from the bottom of the ocean, the world had been in turmoil. Storms every night. Daylight that only barely warranted the name. As though what they had done in bringing an end to the beast had truly meant nothing. It was hard not to see it that way as lightning flashed and the clouds marched forward. The pale pastels of Alice's bedroom did nothing to comfort her. Instead, she felt surrounded and hemmed in by the shiny eyes of the girl's stuffed animals. Getting up, Dale went back into the kitchen.

Ethan was cooking from cans.

He looked up when she entered and gave her a smile.

"Canned beans again, but I found some meat, so it won't be as bad."

Dale nodded and sat down at the table, putting her head in her hands.

"We can't stay here."

"I know." The answer was there almost before she finished speaking. He slopped some food into bowls and put them on the table. "But where are we going to go?"

It had been easier when there had been more of them. Then again, back then, they had a purpose. They were going to save the world. Except they had succeeded and there didn't seem to be much point. The world was still dreary and empty. They had sacrificed everything and for what? To see the storms, roll in and batter down everything.

"I," Dale stopped and let out a sigh. "I don't know. There's nothing here. No one here."

"It's just so empty and the world hasn't changed. I mean, we won, but what did we win?" she continued. "An empty world."

"We won a chance to survive as a species," Ethan said. "So maybe it's time we go on. James would have expected it. Victoria would want it too. And Roger."

Everyone they had lost.

"Do you think that thing let them go?"

It was a dark thought. One they had chosen not to look at truthfully. The chance that maybe even after everything for those who had fallen, things were not truly over.

"I don't know, but its creature is gone. The statue is gone. Certainly, there isn't anything else we have to worry about." Ethan shrugged and shoved a spoon in his bowl. "Eat before it gets cold. It's only a little better warm."

They ate in silence.

"Tomorrow, we'll go. We'll pack what we can and get out of here. Head somewhere sunny and south." Ethan smiled at the thought and Dale made herself smile back. "After all, who says we have to stick around? It's not like it's coming back. And even if it did, who is there up here to influence, but us?"

He was right. The town was empty. No one boating. No one fishing. No chance of that creature's carcass ever being stumbled upon assuming there was anything left once the fish had gotten done with it. The thought of that giant creature being slowly picked apart by a million smaller ones made her smile a little wider. Serves it right.

Senora was still a ghost town when Dale and Ethan put it at their backs and started down the highway, heading south. Last evening's left puddles, and ripped the Welcome to Senora sign down, but otherwise there was little sign of anything being amiss. Just the awareness of a town which was no longer anything more than a shadow of itself, waiting for time to do what it did best.

Reclaim everything.

THE END

ABOUT ALLEDRIA HURT

ALLEDRIA HURT is an African-American author of diverse works. She has written in the realms of Fantasy, Science Fiction, and Horror with nearly 30 published pieces across those genres. When she's not busy writing, she's being a full-time cat mom, an A+ actress, a stellar ghost tour coach, and an on again off again health enthusiast. She can be found on the internet under http://linktr.ee/alledria.

www.ingramcontent.com/pod-product-compliance
Lightning Source LLC
Chambersburg PA
CBHW072228170626
46813CB00003B/1134